KU-168-188

TRIGGER LAW

JACKSON COLE

THORNDIKE
CHIVERS

This Large Print edition is published by Thorndike Press, Waterville, Maine, USA and by BBC Audiobooks Ltd, Bath, England.

Thorndike Press, a part of Gale, Cengage Learning.

The text of this Large Print edition is unabridged.

Other aspects of the book may vary from the original edition.

Set in 16 pt. Plantin.

Printed on permanent paper.

LIBRARY OF CONGRESS CATALOGING-IN-PUBLICATION DATA

Cole, Jackson.
   Trigger law / by Jackson Cole.
     p. cm. — (Thorndike Press large print Western)
     ISBN-13: 978-1-4104-0516-6 (hardcover : alk. paper)
     ISBN-10: 1-4104-0516-8 (hardcover : alk. paper)
     1. Texas — Fiction. 2. Large type books. I. Title.
PS3505.O2685T74 2008
813'.52—dc22
                                     2007046710

BRITISH LIBRARY CATALOGUING-IN-PUBLICATION DATA AVAILABLE

Published in 2008 by arrangement with Golden West Literary Agency.

Published in 2008 in the U.K. by arrangement with Golden West Literary Agency.

U.K. Hardcover: 978 1 405 64476 1 (Chivers Large Print)

U.K. Softcover: 978 1 405 64477 8 (Camden Large Print)

Printed in the United States of America
1 2 3 4 5 6 7 12 11 10 09 08

TRIGGER LAW

1

"Hold it, horse!"

Jim Hatfield snapped the command as Goldy, his great golden sorrel, shied so violently as to almost unseat his tall rider. He glanced down, saw the raised body and head of a sidewinder that had almost fanged the horse with his vicious lateral stroke.

Hatfield's hand flickered down and up. There was a wisp of smoke, and the crash of a report that sent the echoes flying back and forth among the buttes and chimney rocks.

The upreared head suddenly vanished. The upper portion of the decapitated body thrashed and writhed.

Hatfield ejected the spent shell from his Colt and replaced it with a fresh cartridge. His hand paused halfway as he started to thrust the big gun back into its holster. He stared at the dying snake in mild surprise.

The upper half of the body continued to

jerk and quiver with lessening force. But the tail and lower half lay quite motionless on the hot sand.

"Why, the darn thing had a broken back!" he told Goldy. "I thought it was funny for it to be lying out here in the blazing sun. A rattler can't stand much hot sunlight — kills him in a hurry."

Instinctively he glanced keenly about for a solution of the mystery. The hand that held the Colt tensed.

From a clump of sage near what passed for a trail across the Tonto Desert, protruded a moccasin and a stretch of ragged velvet pantaloon.

Hatfield dismounted with lithe grace, still cautious. Anything could happen in this burned over stretch of hell, and usually did. He advanced toward the bush, under which he could now make out a shadowy form.

Abruptly, with an exclamation of pity, he holstered his gun and hurried forward. The ankle showing between moccasin and pantaloon was hideously swollen.

"Snake struck him and he stamped on it and busted its back," Hatfield muttered, pushing his way under the low branches of the sage. He saw now that the man who lay there was a Mexican. The face into which he peered was frightfully cadaverous —

bones under a stretching of leathery dark skin. The body was emaciated. A glance told Hatfield that the man was very old. He was a rather grim-looking specimen and, Hatfield decided, was of almost pure Indian blood.

"Darn near starved," Hatfield muttered. "So weak he couldn't take the venom from even a pygmy rattlesnake. Had just about strength left, I reckon, to stamp on the spotted devil and bust its back before he keeled over and crawled under the sage to get away from the sun."

As Hatfield leaned near, the closed lids flickered, raised a trifle, showing a glint of black eyes.

"Anything I can do?" Hatfield asked in Spanish.

The shrunken lips of the dying man writhed forth a single word —

"Agua!"

Hatfield's own cracked and blackened lips tightened a little, but he did not hesitate. He got his canteen from the saddle pouch and let the last few drops it contained trickle into the Mexican's mouth.

The old man swallowed slowly and painfully until the water was gone. Then he sank back with a deep sigh. Abruptly he looked up.

"All you got?" he asked, speaking a halting English.

Hatfield nodded. "Sorry, but that's all," he replied. "I'll pack you along with me till we find more."

The old Mexican shook his head. "You give all," he muttered in a cracked whisper. "I die. It was *bueno, muy bueno* — much good. But maybe you die too because you give all."

Hatfield smiled, and shrugged his broad shoulders.

"*Quien sabe* — who knows?" he replied. "Don't let it worry you, old timer. We all have to go some day, when our time is up. No use bothering about it till it happens. Now I'm going to take you along with me. Maybe we can find a doctor to look after that leg. Nothing I can do for it — poison has already spread."

Again a negative shake of the white head.

"I die," the Mexican repeated, positively. "You give all. I give all, too."

A claw-like hand thrust inside the ragged shirt, fumbled about and came forth holding something. He thrust the object into Hatfield's hand. Hatfield mechanically grasped it. The object was of metal and astonishingly heavy for its size.

A single death-clouded word writhed past

the Mexican's lips —

"Metzli!"

A choking gasp. Then, in a ready whisper —

"Valle de la Luna!"

The Mexican tried desperately to speak again, striving to say more, but only a choking rattle came forth. His scrawny chest swelled, his body tensed, relaxed. The chest sank in, and did not rise again.

"Poor old feller," Hatfield muttered compassionately. "He's gone." His eyes raised to the brassy-blue sky where a black dot was already whirling and planing.

"And maybe he's not far ahead of me," he muttered, trying to wet his dry lips with an equally dry tongue. His eyes dropped to what he held in his hand and he uttered an astonished exclamation.

The thing was a dull-yellow image about three inches in length by one and a half in thickness. Its weight told Hatfield it could be nothing but solid gold. A point of stone had been worked into the base and the stone showed a clean but weathered fracture. Evidently the image had been torn away from a stone pedestal or other support.

The face that surmounted the squat body of the image was fiendish in expression.

Above the low forehead was fashioned a peculiar head-dress in the form of a crescent. The eyes were as large as Hatfield's fingertip, and acrawl with strange and vari-colored fires.

"Opals!" Hatfield muttered. "Mexican opals, sure as shootin' — the bad luck stones. Now what in blazes? 'Metzli,' the old jigger said. Unless I'm remembering wrong, Metzli was the Aztec moon god. The particular deity of the miners and metal workers. What else was that he said — Valle de la Luna — Valley of the Moon. If this isn't the darndest thing!"

Shaking his head in bewilderment, he straightened up and turned around — to gaze squarely into the muzzle of a gun!

Behind the gun was a man, a lean, lanky man with a dark face and lashless looking eyes of pale gray. Absorbed as he had been in the dying Mexican and his singular bequest, even the keen ears of Jim Hatfield had not detected his stealthy approach across the soft sands.

"I'll take it, feller," he growled in a harsh, menacing voice.

"Take what?" Hatfield asked, sparring for time.

"The thing yuh got in your hand," said the other — "the image the old hellion give

12

yuh. I'll take it."

The gun jutted forward threateningly as he spoke.

But the man a stern old Lieutenant of Rangers had named the Lone Wolf was not an easy man to get the drop on.

"Okay, take it," Hatfield said, thrusting the image toward the gunman.

The other instinctively reached. The barrel of his gun wavered a trifle.

Hatfield's hand shot forward. The heavy lump of gold spun through the air and caught the other squarely between his pale eyes. The gun roared, but Hatfield was going sideways at the same instant. His own Colt fairly leaped from the holster.

But there was no need to use it. The gunman lay sprawled on the sand, completely out.

Hatfield instinctively stooped to recover the image. As he did so, something yelled through the space his body had occupied the instant before. The image grasped in his left hand, he whirled sideways again, and swore angrily.

Riding toward him shooting and yelling, and not more than three hundred yards distant, were fully a dozen more men.

Hatfield did not hesitate. He thrust the image into his pocket, holstered his gun and forked Goldy all in the same coordination of movement. Odds of twelve to one were a mite heavy for even Captain Bill McDowell's Lieutenant and ace-man. He was sure that the old Commander of The Border Battalion would himself have felt that such close association with a band of degraded owlhoots would be contaminating, and would have proceeded to remove himself from their neighborhood as speedily as possible.

With lead hissing all around him, Goldy seemed thoroughly in accord with his master. He proceeded to go away from there and go away fast. Hatfield leaned low in the saddle and urged him on with voice and hand. He was not particularly worried, for shooting at such a distance from the back of a racing horse was little more than guesswork, and aside from a chance unlucky hit, he had little to fear. And he was confident that Goldy's great speed and endurance would quickly distance the pursuit.

Swiftly the great sorrel drew away from the wrathful pursuers. Bullets ceased to come close, and in another few minutes the firing ceased altogether. Hatfield straightened in the saddle and settled himself comfortably. Then for a second time he uttered a wrathful exclamation.

Ahead and to the right, swooping along on a slant that would cut the fugitive's trail, was another body of horsemen. Hatfield counted four. What a moment before had been but irritating, abruptly became deadly serious.

Instinctively, Hatfield veered to the left. A moment later he glanced back and saw that the pursuit had gained a little.

"Cut over enough to clear that bunch ahead, and the main outfit will catch up with me," he muttered. "They'll be riding the short leg of the triangle."

He gazed longingly ahead to where, shadowy against the skyline, loomed dark, craggy hills slashed with canyons and draws. They were not so very far off, but the speeding horsemen riding down the long slant from the west were much nearer, and drawing closer with every racing stride.

Nearer loomed the hills, but the four hard riding horsemen had gained appreciably. Bullets began whining past again. The pursuers behind had cut his advantage by almost half. Hatfield glanced back at them, glanced ahead, and uttered an exclamation. Instinctively his hand tightened on the bridle.

Straight ahead, where the four horsemen were charging down a long slope, the ground abruptly fell away — fell away to a wide bench fifteen feet below, then plunged in a dizzy slant to the floor of a gloomy canyon that zigzagged toward the eastern tip of the hills. To ride down that boulder strewn sag appeared to be nothing but madness. But Hatfield instantly made up his mind.

"You haven't got wings, horse, but you'd better grow them," he told Goldy. "Okay, feller, it's up to you."

But it was up to Hatfield first. The four horsemen reached the drop first, scant yards ahead of the racing horseman. Their guns blazed. But their horses were wild with excitement. They snorted and plunged, and before their riders could quiet them, Hatfield's voice rang out like a golden bugle call of sound —

"Trail, Goldy, trail!"

The great sorrel shot forward in a soaring bound. Hatfield's guns flamed and thundered. Straight into the milling group charged the sorrel. There was a crackling roar of shots, a pandemonium of flying lead, plunging horses and yelling men as Goldy landed in the tangle like a thunderbolt.

Down went two horses, their riders cursing and screaming. A third man spun from his saddle as Hatfield's guns blazed right in his face. Goldy crashed into the fourth horse as he carromed sideways off the first two. Hatfield had a fleeting glimpse of a rage distorted face and two blazing dark eyes as horse and rider went to the ground in a sprawling tangle.

Over the lip soared Goldy, as if he actually had "growed" wings. He hit the bench, stumbled, floundered, regained his footing with cat-like agility and went storming down the slope accompanied by a cloud of dust and an avalanche of loosened boulders. Hatfield swaying easily in the saddle, kept his head up and encouraged him with voice and hand. Goldy snorted response and sped the faster.

On the lip above, the larger band of horsemen had joined their fellows. The big black-eyed man, apparently the leader of the bunch, cursed and raged at his mounted followers, profanely ordering them over the edge in pursuit of the Ranger. But the horses refused to take the jump and their riders were not particularly enthusiastic in urging them on.

Bullets hissed and crackled through the air, but Goldy was far down the slope now and going like the wind. Nor did the boiling dust cloud that accompanied his progress make for accurate shooting. A moment later he hit the canyon floor with a clang of clashing irons and went speeding down the shadowy gorge.

Glancing over his shoulder, Hatfield saw that the horsemen were streaming purposefully northward along the canyon rim at a fast pace. He faced to the front and urged Goldy to greater speed.

"Looks like they know just where they're going," he muttered. "Chances are there's an easy way into this crack, farther up. Well, they won't have much chance running us down. It'll be dark in a little while, and Goldy will hold his lead without any trouble. June along, horse, we got places to go. Looks like other gents have gone through here from time to time, too. Lots of hoof prints, nearly all heading south."

2

Hatfield rode down the canyon in a very wrathful mood. He had not liked being chased like a sheep-killing coyote.

"Sure wish I'd got a better look at that black-eyed jigger," he growled. "I've a prime notion he's the he-wolf of the pack. But about all I saw clear was his eyes. I wouldn't recognize him if I met him in the middle of the trail. Seemed sort of tall.

"It all comes from trying for a short-cut across that blasted stretch of desert," he told Goldy. "First we get plumb lost in a sand storm, then we come nigh to getting snake-bit, and then we tangle with a whole pack of sidewinders. Right now we're lost again. No way of telling where this darn crack through the hills leads to. Anyhow, though, it 'pears to head in the general direction we figured to go — south by east a mite."

A moment later he uttered a thankful exclamation. Directly ahead, gushing from under a cliff, was a spring of clear water. In a split second he and the sorrel were both downing the first decent drink they had had in nearly twenty-four hours.

Finally, with a long sigh of satisfaction, Hatfield sat back on his heels, fished the makin's from his pocket and began rolling a cigarette with the slim fingers of his left hand. From force of long habit, he studied his surroundings minutely, casting glances back the way they had come although he had little fear of pursuit catching up with him.

"Chances are those jiggers got a skinful," he decided. "None of 'em 'peared to want to follow up when we went down the sag. And from the looks of this hole, there's no chance of anybody scooting on ahead and cutting us off. The walls are straight-up-and-down, and we're already getting into the hills. Hope the darn thing doesn't turn out to be a box, or we'll have a nice long ride back to somewhere we can get out. Let's see how much damage has been done."

The damage turned out to be slight. Hatfield found two holes in the crown of his hat, another through the brim. Still another passing slug had bored his shirt sleeve and drawn a few drops of blood from his arm as it burned the flesh. A fifth had nicked his chaps where they flared out from his holster. But otherwise he was untouched. Goldy hadn't lost a patch of hair.

Hatfield smoked in comfort for a few minutes in the shade of the cliff overhang. Then he remembered the curious image that, it seemed, had started the shindig. He drew the thing from his pocket, hefted it and looked it over carefully. He shook his black head in a puzzled fashion.

"What in blazes is this all about?" he demanded of the image. "Were those sidewinders trying to run down that old Mexican for this thing? Looks sort of like it. They were scattered all over the section like a brush combing bunch would be. And the one who snuk up on me and braced me sure knew just what he was after. But why? This thing is worth some dinero, all right. There's a few ounces of gold here, and the stones may be even more valuable than the metal. Hard to tell about that. Takes an expert to accurately appraise Mexican opals. But even if they're stones of the first water, there isn't enough value here to warrant a bunch of fifteen or sixteen taking a chance on that desert to run this thing down. Sure doesn't make sense. But to all appearances this is what they were after, and they were willing to go in for a killing and risk eating lead themselves to get it."

His long, black-lashed eyes of a peculiar shade of green hardened as he thought of the men who had thrown lead at him.

"May have been a legitimate outfit after what they figured belonged to them," he mused, "but I don't think so. They had all the earmarks of an owlhoot bunch. I've a notion they'll bear a mite of investigating, if I ever get where I can do some investigating. Wonder if there is any tie-up with what Captain Bill sent me over here for?"

Sparse grass grew on the banks of the little stream that flowed from the spring. Hatfield removed the bit from Goldy's mouth and allowed him to graze for a few minutes. While the horse was cropping grass, he sat down and drew a letter from his pocket, a letter he had received while attending to some routine Ranger business at the eastern arc of the Big Bend country.

A mite east of where you are now (Captain Bill wrote) is a cow and mining town called Sanders. I got a note from a fellow living in that section, a fellow named Walt Cowdry. I knew him pretty well back in the old days. He writes that they're having a heap of trouble with a bunch he calls Roma's

22

Raiders. Chances are it will turn out to be just some sort of a petty widelooping outfit that can well be taken care of by the local authorities. But seeing as it's not far from where you are at present, suppose you amble over to Sanders for a looksee. Tell Cowdry hello for me when you see him. He was a 'good Injun' when him and me worked together for the old Slash K outfit. Understand he's gotten pretty well off since then. Writes his brand burn is Cross C with an over-bit ear-mark.

Complying with Captain Bill's request, Hatfield had headed for where he had been told Sanders was located. To save time, he attempted to skirt a strip of arid desert with disastrous results. He knew, however, that he could not be far from the country for which he was headed.

It was Captain Bill McDowell who had been responsible for Jim Hatfield becoming a Ranger. Some years before, just after Hatfield had graduated from engineering college, his father had been ruthlessly murdered by wideloopers. Young Jim, his heart black with hatred, had resolved to avenge his father's death. But just as he was setting out, Captain McDowell had summoned him to his office.

"I know how you feel, Jim," said the Grand Old Man of the Rangers, "but I also know what you're letting yourself in for. When a man takes the law into his own hands, he's skirting mighty close to outlaw land no matter how justified he may feel. It's just a little slip, then you're in the same corral with the jiggers you're after. Too big a risk to take, Jim."

"I don't propose to let the devils get away with it," Hatfield grimly responded. "Dad wouldn't sleep easy in his grave if I did."

Captain McDowell nodded. "But there are ways, and ways," he said. "I'm offering you the right way. Come into the Rangers, Jim. The first chore I'll hand you is running those skunks down. You'll have the law on your side and the support of all honest men. That's the right way to do it. What do you say?"

Hatfield considered, then he said slowly, "I say, suh, you've hired yourself a hand."

"Of course," added the crafty old Captain, "after the chore is finished, you can get out of the service and go ahead with your engineering. It's a bargain."

Captain Bill would have kept his side of the bargain, but the chase proved long and arduous. Jim Hatfield brought his father's killers to justice, but before the chore was finished he knew he had found his life work. He was a Ranger!

And now the Lone Wolf was a legend. Captain Bill's Lieutenant and ace-man, and his exploits, were talked of from end to end of Texas and beyond. Hated and feared by the owlhoot brand; admired and respected by honest men.

It was gratefully cool in the canyon's depths after the blazing glare of the desert, but Hatfield did not care to linger long by the spring. He hadn't forgotten the purposeful way the owlhoots rode north along the canyon rim. The sky was reddening with approaching sunset when he tightened his cinches and rode on down the canyon.

"You've filled up, after a fashion," he told Goldy, "but I'm so empty I'd boom like a drum if anybody hit me. June along, horse, let's see if we can find a place where folks eat something besides wind pudding."

On and on the canyon wound through the hills, with the little stream, increased by several additional springs, now flowing through the center of the brush grown floor. The depths were shadowy and along the lofty rim played strange and glorious fires as the lower edge of the sun dipped beneath the western crags. Soon these died to a tremulous glow. The strip of sky burned scarlet and primrose, softened to a dusty pink that paled to pearly gray and then deepened again to violet. Needlepoints of flame that were stars appeared as the violet changed in turn to purply-black.

Hatfield slowed Goldy's pace. He no longer had any fear of pursuit. Besides, it had become very dark in the narrow gorge and he didn't care to risk the sorrel's legs on the boulder strewn surface.

Another twenty minutes of cautious progress and the Lone Wolf exclaimed with relief. They had rounded a turn and before them, less than a mile distant lay a cluster of "fallen stars" glowing through the darkness. They could be no other than the lights of a town. Ten minutes more and Hatfield was conscious of a deep and monotonous humming that, as he proceeded, loudened to a grinding rumble.

"Stamp mills!" he exclaimed. "Big ones, too. Horse, I've a plumb notion we're coming to that town of Sanders we've been hunting for. We were told it was located in a canyon mouth. Uh-huh, can't be anything else. We got a break. The way we were going when that shindig started, we might have over-run it by miles."

Goldy, scenting the possibility of oats and

a comfortable stall, quickened his pace.

Soon they were passing through the straggling outskirts of the town which sat in the canyon mouth. The east wall of the gorge fairly shadowed the crooked main street, while the west wall fell away to give place to a vista of rolling rangeland with the granite claws of the hills extending forward to form canyons and gulches. Farther westward and to the south were mountains, darker shadows on the shadowy skyline, which Hatfield knew must be the peaks of the Bullis Gap Range. And there to the southwest was owl-hoot country of the worst sort. "Wet" cows came across the Rio Grande there, and smuggler trains and gents who found *manana* land too hot to hold them.

"And this pueblo is situated just about right to be a lay-over point for that kind," was the Lone Wolf's unerring diagnosis.

Past the shadowy bulk of the stamp mills, Hatfield rode. Then came long rows of cattle-loading pens flanking a railroad siding. Further to the south, beyond the jutting bulge of the west canyon wall, gleamed the twin steel rails of the railroad main line, with a station squatting beside the tracks.

But between the stamp mills and the railroad was the heart of the town, a crooked main street lined with shacks, dobes and false fronts, with here and there a two-story "skyscraper" rising grandly above the common level. Lanterns hung on poles at the corners provided inadequate street lighting, which, however, was abetted by golden bars of radiance streaming through the windows of stores, saloons, dance halls and gambling places. Long rows of hitchracks lined the board sidewalk, and Hatfield noted plenty of cow ponies tethered to the pegs. Evidently the town did considerable outside business.

Hatfield hitched Goldy at a convenient rack and pushed through the swinging doors of a saloon whose sign declared prime food was available on the premises as well as liquid refreshment.

The big room was pretty well crowded and a babble of talk set the hanging lamps to flickering. Almost instantly, however, it died to a hum, then ceased altogether. As Hatfield approached the bar he was conscious of eyes resting on him from every direction.

"Whe-e-ew!" he whistled to himself. "Strangers sure get a prime going over in this pueblo."

Apparently oblivious of the rather unnerving reception, he unconcernedly ordered a drink, tossed it off and ordered another, which he sipped. The bartender served him in silence, then moved away to relieve the wants of an equally silent patron.

Gradually, however, the talk resumed, though Hatfield felt that those near him spoke in guarded tones. In the back bar mirror he surveyed the room and its occupants.

He decided that the patrons were about equally divided between miners and cowhands. Some of the former doubtless found employment in the stamp mills whose grumble ceaselessly jarred the air. And some of the men in cow country dress, Hatfield felt sure, could show no recent marks of rope or branding iron.

"Yes, she's a lay-over point, all right," he reiterated his former diagnosis of the town. "I've a notion quite a few of those gents at the bar and the tables do most of their riding between sunset and sunrise."

"How's the chuck over to the lunch counter?" he asked the barkeep.

"Fair to middlin'," the drink juggler replied in cordial enough tones. "We aim to serve the best in town, and we don't have many complaints. Feller come in here the other day and ordered two fried eggs, one fried on one side and one fried on the other. That started an argfyin' in the kitchen between the waiter and the cook, but the gent finally compromised on havin' 'em scrambled and 'lowed they was okay."

This bit of interesting information was accompanied by a frightful contortion of the barkeep's countenance which, Hatfield deduced, was intended for a wink. He smiled and the bartender moved off chuckling.

Hatfield was about to seek the lunch counter and risk the argumentative cook and waiter, when abruptly the talk in the room fell flat again. He glanced around to ascertain the cause.

Coming through the door was a tall man who paused to glance around, smiling thinly. His eyes, now slightly narrowed, Hatfield noted were a very dark blue. His features were good, his mouth tight-lipped. After the instant of hesitation, he headed for the bar, walking with long, lithe strides and casting contemptuous glances from side to side. Hatfield noted his clothes were powdered with desert dust.

There was a vacant spot next to where Hatfield stood, and the new arrival occupied it. The bartender hurried to serve him, but poured the drink in silence. It seemed to Hatfield that his hand shook a little as he tipped the bottle over the glass.

The other downed his drink and called

for another which was likewise poured in silence.

This time the conversation in the room was slower to resume, and it seemed to Hatfield it did not reach its former tone and freedom.

The man beside him seemed to sense this also, for the sarcastic smile on his thin lips widened a little and his darkly blue eyes narrowed a trifle more.

Abruptly he turned to face Hatfield. "Stranger here, aren't yuh?" he asked in a deep voice.

"Just landed," Hatfield admitted.

"I ain't," the other replied, adding with a bitter twist of his lips, "but I might as well be. Fact is, I reckon I shouldn't be talkin' to you. It won't do yuh any good hereabouts."

Hatfield glanced down at him. The other was a tall man, six feet and a little more, but he had to raise his gaze a little to meet the Lone Wolf's level green eyes.

"Feller, I choose my own company," the Ranger replied, "and I haven't heard myself asking you to move along."

The other stared, but the grin that followed the stare had nothing of contempt in it.

"Much obliged," he said. "My name's Kells, Hugh Kells."

Hatfield supplied his own name, and they shook hands. And it seemed to Hatfield that the hum of conversation again assumed a lower note.

"Have a drink?" Kells asked.

"Was just going to put on the nosebag, but I reckon I can stand another," Hatfield accepted. "Got my throat pretty well lined with desert dust today. Rode over from the west."

"West of the Tonto?" the other asked, incredulously. "Yuh mean to say yuh crossed that section of flattened out hell at this time of the year?"

"Reckon I did," Hatfield replied, adding with a smile that flashed his even teeth startlingly white in his bronzed face, "but I reckon I won't try it again."

"You were loco to try it once," the other said. "If a sand storm had caught up with you, yuh wouldn't be here tellin' me about it."

"One did," Hatfield replied, "but I got a pretty good horse and he pulled me through it."

"He must be a lulu," Kells declared with conviction.

"You live hereabouts?" Hatfield asked as they raised their glasses.

"Calc'late to have for the past two years,"

32

admitted Kells.

"Maybe you may have heard of a gent named Cowdry, Walt Cowdry, then," Hatfield remarked. "A feller I know told me he knew him, just before I headed over in this direction. Feller said he owns a ranch — the Cross C — somewhere hereabouts. Figured I might look him up."

"Well, if yuh do, yuh'll take a longer and maybe a hotter trip than yuh did across the Tonto Desert," Kells replied grimly.

"How's that?" Hatfield asked.

"Because he's dead and buried," Kells replied. "Old Walt Cowdry got hisself killed last week, drygulched from the brush."

3

It was Hatfield's turn to stare. Before he could reply, the swinging doors suddenly banged open and an enormously fat man came charging in.

As the new arrival paused just inside the door, Hatfield noted that he had wide-spreading walrus mustaches, twinkling little gray eyes, a red button of a nose and pursed lips. On his sagging vest was pinned a big nickel badge that said "Sheriff" in no uncertain terms. Against his right thigh, a holstered gun hung in a very business-like manner.

The sheriff glared about suspiciously. His eyes centered on Hatfield and he came waddling across to the bar.

"Where'd you come from?" he demanded, with a profane qualification as to the general region.

"Another place," Hatfield replied instantly.

"What's that?" barked the sheriff.

"Another place," Hatfield repeated. "You evidently got it figured I don't come from this place, so it must be from another place."

The sheriff turned purple and appeared to breathe with difficulty.

"Listen," he snorted, "I asked yuh a civil question and I expect a civil answer."

"Yes," Hatfield agreed mildly, "you asked a civil question, but you didn't ask it in a very civil way."

The sheriff seemed slightly taken aback.

"It's my business to ask questions," he growled. "For all I know, you might be Roma hisself."

"Gosh! that helps!" Kells broke in. "I figered everybody around here thinks I am Roma."

The sheriff whirled on him.

"Nobody's accused you of bein' Roma," he retorted.

"No, not to my face," Kells replied grimly, "but there's talk been goin' around and you know it, Sheriff Walsh."

"If yuh were more pertickler as to who yuh associate with, folks wouldn't be talkin'," the sheriff returned meaningly.

"Who's Roma?" Hatfield interrupted at this point.

"He's a blankety-blank owlhoot that had ought to be dancin' at the end of a rope on nothing," declared the sheriff.

Hatfield turned to Kells.

"Blazes, feller," he remarked seriously. "Looks like you and I are sort of on a spot."

"Oh, shut up, dadblame yuh!" swore the sheriff. "There's too many lippy younkers showin' up here of late. Anybody might be Roma. I might be him myself, if I weighed a hundred pounds or so less and was twenty years younger, from all anybody's been able to find out about the hellion."

Hatfield chuckled. "Have a snort, Sheriff," he invited. "That is if you don't mind drinking with a couple of owlhoots." He smiled down at the irritated old peace officer, his sternly handsome face of a sudden wonderfully pleasing.

In spite of himself, the sheriff had to grin in return.

"Everybody's jumpy hereabouts of late," he explained apologetically. "Let a stranger a mite out of the ordinary show up, and somebody comes hightailin' to tell me he figgers Roma's just rode into town. I wish the sidewinder would ride in, and give us a chance to line sights with him!"

"You don't know what he looks like, then?" Hatfield asked as the bartender poured.

"No," the sheriff admitted. "Nobody does.

He shows here and he shows there, wide-loops a herd, holds up a stage, busts open a bank and is gone like a jackrabbit into the brush. If he ain't the devil, he's his first cousin."

"A bunch can't hold up a stage or rob a bank without somebody getting a look at them," Hatfield objected.

"Roma don't usually leave no witnesses," the Sheriff replied grimly. "And his bunch always operates masked."

Hatfield nodded, his eyes thoughtful.

"How many usually in his bunch?" he asked.

"The few times they been spotted, there's usually a dozen or more," said the sheriff, sucking the drops from his mustache.

Hatfield nodded again, looking even more thoughtful.

"I'm sort of in line for a small surrounding," he announced. "You gents care to join me?"

"Not a bad notion," Kells agreed.

"I ain't et for about an hour; reckon I can stand a helpin'," said the sheriff.

Curious glances were shot at the three as they sat down together at the table, but no comments were made that Hatfield could catch.

Hatfield had not eaten for twenty-four

hours and he put away a splendid dinner, but the sheriff far exceeded his finest efforts. Hatfield couldn't but help wondering what he would have stowed away if he hadn't "et" for *two* hours.

Finally the sheriff shoved back his plate with a deep sigh.

"That's better," he said. "Ain't good to go empty too long. Sort of makes a feller get on the prod too easy. Well, reckon I'd better amble back to the office. Roma is liable to ride in again any minute."

"Know a place where I can put up my horse and knock off a mite of shut-eye?" Hatfield asked.

"Turn to the right when yuh go out the door," said the sheriff. "Then right around the next corner is a livery stable that's okay. A Mexican runs it, but he's a good oiler. He has a couple of rooms to rent, over the stalls, if yuh like to sleep close to your horse. They're clean, and no bugs, which is more than yuh can say for most of the flea sacks in this pueblo. Tell him I sent yuh."

With a nod, he rolled away from the table and out the door. Kells chuckled, and pinched out the butt of his cigarette.

"Walsh is okay," he said. "He don't give a blank what anybody says or thinks. Makes up his own mind and sticks by it. A heap saltier than yuh'd think to look at him. Lots of muscle under that fat, and the way he can handle a gun is something to ride a long ways to see. If he ever does line sights with Roma, it'll be too bad for that owlhoot. Well, I got to be amblin' myself. Got a few miles to ride."

"Live in the neighborhood?" Hatfield asked.

"Sort of," Kells replied. "My little spread, the Tumbling K, is in a big wide canyon over to the east — prime range. It's called Moon Valley."

Hatfield's face did not change expression, but his eyes seemed to lighten a trifle till the green was almost gray.

"I'll be back in town tomorrow," Kells added as he got to his feet. "You figger on coilin' your twine hereabouts for a spell?"

"I may, if I can tie onto a job of riding or something," Hatfield replied.

Kells looked interested. "Know anything about minin'?" he asked suddenly.

"A little," Hatfield admitted.

"I'll be in here about noon tomorrow," Kells said. "Sure would like to have a mite of talk with you then if you're still here."

"I'll be here," Hatfield said definitely.

"Okay, I'll see yuh then," Kells said. With a nod he turned and crossed the room with lithe strides and vanished into the darkness. Hatfield rolled another cigarette and sat smoking thoughtfully.

" *'Valle de la Luna,'* was the last words that dying Mexican said," he mused. "And into plain Texan, that translates very nicely — Moon Valley. Now what in blazes am I tangled with, anyhow? Roma's Riders! Sounds like a brush sliding widelooping bunch. But it appears they're considerable more than that. Poor old Walt Cowdry. 'Pears he wasn't talking through his hat when he wrote that letter to Captain Bill. And the sheriff, who looks to be a capable old jigger, admits he's plumb up against it. Looks like I'm in for an interesting time in this section."

A smile of pleased anticipation quirked his rather wide mouth as he dwelt on a situation that could well give even the Lone Wolf pause.

"I'm playing a great big hunch that the bunch who chased me today were the Roma's Riders outfit," he continued his reflections. "If so, it 'pears I'm about the only jigger mavericking around who ever got a look at the hellions and lived to talk about it, judging from what the sheriff said. May be wrong, of course, but I figgered that big black-eyed gent was giving the orders. If so, he must be Roma. I wouldn't recognize him if I saw him, but I have got a notion of his general appearance. 'Peared to have black eyes, all right.

"But," he added thoughtfully a moment later, "dark blue eyes look black at times. Moon Valley! I wonder!"

He pinched out his cigarette and stood up, stretching his long arms above his head. The babble of talk did not lessen as he sauntered across the room to the door. Apparently association with Sheriff Walsh had dissipated any suspicion that might have been directed toward him when he first put in an appearance.

Unhitching Goldy, he walked to the corner and turned into an alley. The livery stable was situated but a few yards from its mouth. Light glowed through chinks in the heavy door. A knock brought an alert looking young Mexican to answer the summons.

"Sheriff said you could put up me and the cayuse tonight," Hatfield explained.

The Mexican smiled with a flash of white teeth.

"Sheriff Walsh is *bueno hombre*," he said.

"Uh-huh, 'pears to be a good man, especially with a knife and fork," Hatfield agreed.

"One need not take shame to his own appetite when the *Senor* Walsh sits at table with him," the other chuckled. "*Senor,* I am Tomaso, at your service."

He opened the door wide. Hatfield led Goldy into the stable.

"The *caballo magnifico!*" exclaimed Tomaso, gazing with sparkling eyes at the great sorrel. "We will place him in the stall here by the window, *Senor.* It is cooler there."

He reached out an unhesitating hand to Goldy's bridle iron. The sorrel shot him a questioning glance, then followed without protest.

"You've got a way with horses all right, Tomaso," Hatfield said. "Old Goldy isn't much on letting strangers touch him. Okay, I'll let you look after him. You'll know what to do. And can I have a place to sleep, too?"

"The room at the head of the stairs, *Senor.* There also is the large window. I sleep at the far end of the hall, should you wish anything during the night. The bracket lamp on the wall burns all night, so should you wish to descend the stairs, you will not fall. And here is a key to the door, should you decide to leave for some purpose. I do not usually provide keys, but the *amigo* of the *Senor* Walsh, that is different."

Hatfield thanked the Mexican keeper and ascended to the room assigned him. It was small, opening onto a narrow hallway that was boarded off from the haymow in the rear, but it was spotlessly clean and the narrow bunk built against the wall looked comfortable. A curtained window opened onto the alley through which blew a pleasantly cool breeze.

Tomaso lighted the wall lamp and with a courteous *"buenos noches, Senor,"* departed to seek his own rest.

Despite the wearying day he had undergone, Hatfield did not immediately go to bed. He drew off his boots, placed the one chair in the room beside the window and sat down. He rolled a cigarette and smoked for a while. Then he sat with his elbows on the window sill, enjoying the cool breeze and gazing across the flat roof of a shack on the opposite side of the alley toward where the lighting of the main street cast a dim glow against the cliff face beyond. The alley was dark save where a corner pole-lantern shot a feeble beam along the base of the opposite buildings.

After a while, Hatfield leaned back in his chair and reached for the makin's again. But his hand abruptly paused as it touched his shirt pocket. On the far side of the alley he had sensed, rather than seen, movement. An instant later a shadowy something outlined into the form of a man standing at the edge of the bar of faint radiance, apparently gazing upward at the open window. Another moment and a second shadowy form joined the first and also stood in a peering attitude.

As Hatfield watched, tense and alert, the two shadows drifted silently across the alley and disappeared in the gloom of the stable wall. To the ears of the rigid watcher above drifted a faint scratching and shuffling sound.

Hatfield eased out of his chair and crossed the room on silent feet. He gently opened the door and glided into the hallway, closing the door behind him.

The hall was empty. The wall lamp, turned low, cast a faint glow across the stair head. Hatfield slipped along the wall and paused at the top step, peering and listening. An instant later he very nearly fell down the stair.

From the depths below knifed a scream, the vicious scream of an angry horse. It was echoed by a howl of pain that didn't come from a horse's throat. In the raging scream, Hatfield recognized Goldy's piercing note. He went down the steps three at a time.

A stream of fire gushed through the window beside the front stall. Hatfield felt the wind of the passing bullet, heard it thud against the wall beside him as the gun roared. His hand streaked to his holster. He blazed three shots at the window square, aiming high lest he strike the horse. An answering slug whined past. Goldy screamed again, more angrily than before. Hatfield heard a curse and the pad of running feet. He leaped to the door, fumbled frantically with the lock.

It took precious seconds to get the door unlocked. He flung it open, dodging back in the same move. From across the alley came another bullet that missed him by scant inches. Both his guns let go with a rattling crash, raking the alley back and forth. He paused, thumbs hooked over the hammers, and listened. He thought he heard a scuffling and scraping on the far side of the alley, but he could see nothing. He waited a moment, then streaked across the open space, weaving and ducking.

No more gunfire answered the move. He flattened against the wall of the shack opposite the stable and listened. Then he groped his way cautiously along the wall.

Almost immediately he came to a narrow opening between two buildings. He peered into it and could see a glow of light flowing across a vacant lot. Nobody was in sight.

He tried to edge into the opening, but his broad shoulders and deep chest couldn't quite make it.

"Must have been a pair of thin jiggers if they went through here," he muttered, "and I don't see where else they could have gone to get out of sight so fast."

He turned around, holstering his guns. From the dark cavern of the stable came an ominous double click. Hatfield found himself staring into the enormous twin muzzles of a ten-gauge shotgun.

"The hands raise!" said a familiar voice.

4

"Hold it, Tomaso!" Hatfield called. "Every-thing's under control. Put that scattergun down before you blow over a house."

"Ah, it is you, *Senor,*" replied Tomaso, stepping into view. "What happened? It sounded as if all the devils of *Infierno* were loose on holiday."

"Somebody tried to climb in the window over there," Hatfield told him. "I reckon Goldy nipped him, judging from the way he yelled."

"So!" growled Tomaso. "They would try to steal the caballo! I wish I could have brought the *escopeta* into play."

"Lucky you didn't," Hatfield replied, with conviction. "You'd have wrecked half the town with that cannon. It had ought to be on wheels."

Men were peering cautiously down the al-ley from the street. A moment later Sheriff Walsh waddled into view, puffing like a freight engine.

"Where's the body?" he demanded.

"Isn't any," Hatfield told him cheerfully. "They got away."

"Too bad," said the sheriff. "There'd ought to be two or three, from all that shootin'. You woke up the whole town. Horse thieves, eh? Gettin' so nothin' is safe hereabouts. Get a look at 'em?"

Hatfield shook his head. "Keep your eyes skun for a jigger short a hunk of meat," he advised the sheriff. "I've a notion my horse left teeth marks on him."

"Pity he hadn't got him by the neck," snorted the sheriff. "Well, I think I'll go eat and then get back to bed."

"A good notion," Hatfield agreed. "I'm going to do the same — the second part, anyhow."

"Better come and eat," urged the sheriff. "Yuh'll need to keep your strength up if yuh hang around in this section. All right, you fellers, bust it up. Everything's quiet."

He stamped back up the alley, herding the crowd before him. Hatfield and Tomaso returned to the stable and shut and locked the door.

"Tomorrow I bar that window with iron," declared Tomaso. "Had I not better sit up and keep watch with the *escopeta?*"

"Oh, they won't come back again tonight," Hatfield replied with conviction. "Let's go to bed."

"Keeps me busy cleaning guns," he growled as he sat down on the bunk and went to work on his Colts. "Well, those hellions didn't waste any time. And they sure are anxious to get hold of that devil-faced hunk of gold. This thing just doesn't make sense. That's what they were after, all right, not the horse. They spotted my window and figured to snuk up on me while I was asleep. Might have done it, too, if it wasn't for Goldy. Me being awake and spotting them was just a bit of luck."

There was no doubt in his mind but that the marauding pair were members of the gang he had the run-in with on the desert. Doubtless they had slid down the canyon, as he suspected they would, in order to reach the town in the canyon mouth. And they would know that Hatfield would of necessity end up in Sanders by way of the canyon.

"But that doesn't explain how they knew right where to find me," he told himself grimly as he holstered his guns and prepared for bed.

Hatfield slept late the following morning. Sunlight was pouring through the window

49

when he awoke. After a shave and a sluice in the trough of cold water in the back of the stable, he ambled out in search of some breakfast. On the corner he met Sheriff Walsh.

"Howdy?" said the sheriff. "Any more trouble? Nope? Well, then, come on and let's eat."

While they were waiting for the food to prepare, Hugh Kells entered the saloon, glanced about, and walked over to their table.

"Set and eat," invited the sheriff. "I done had my breakfast, but I didn't want Hatfield to be lonesome, so I'm havin' a mite of a snack with him. Better make that five eggs for me, waiter, and a double helpin' of ham."

While they ate, Hatfield carefully studied Kells. He certainly did not act or appear like a man who had attempted murder not twelve hours before and was now sitting at a table with his intended victim. But he was the only person other than the sheriff who knew for a certainty where Hatfield intended spending the night.

"Of course," the Lone Wolf mused, "some jigger might have overheard what the sheriff said to me, although nobody was standing close to the table at the time. Also, it wasn't impossible that I was tailed to the livery stable. After all, I haven't a thing on him. A big jigger with his clothes covered with desert dust and with dark blue eyes that could easily be mistaken for black. But that isn't enough to really fasten suspicion on a feller. Wouldn't be surprised if there are quite a few men in the section who could answer that description fairly well. We'll just wait and see which way the pickle squirts."

Sheriff Walsh finished his ham and eggs first. "Got a chore to do," he said, and lumbered out. Hatfield and Kells rolled cigarettes and sat smoking in silence which the latter finally broke.

"How'd yuh like to ride out to my place with me?" he suggested. Hatfield considered. The offer had certain attractions, and just as definite drawbacks. He reflected, however, that Kells would hardly lead him into a trap with the whole town knowing they had ridden off together. Sheriff Walsh would be asking questions if he, Hatfield, did not appear again, questions that would be hard to answer.

"Okay," he agreed. "Reckon it isn't a bad notion. Nothing to do right now."

"I want to talk to you," Kells elaborated, "and want to show you something that may interest you. All set? Let's go."

Hatfield got his horse. They rode out of town, circled the canyon wall and headed east. To the south was rangeland, rolling toward the Rio Grande. To the west the hills sent out long granite claws with narrow, grass grown valleys between them. To the east, the vista was much the same. The wide canyons were grass grown and dotted with chaparral. Far beyond, Hatfield could see where the hills petered out to the east to give way to more rolling prairie.

"A good looking country," he observed to Kells.

"Yes," replied the other. "Fine cow country, though a mite hard to work. Plenty of minerals in the hills, too. Over to the west are half a dozen paying mines. They have their stamps in Sanders."

They had covered perhaps half of the five miles Kells said was the distance to his ranchhouse when they observed a horseman riding toward them at a swift pace. As he drew nearer, Hatfield saw that he was a young man, slender with the steely slenderness of an unsheathed rapier blade, about six feet tall and finely formed. His face reminded Hatfield of a medallion he had once seen of the Roman Emperor Tiberius Caesar. There was the dark hair curling over the broad forehead, the large well opened eyes of cold gray, the powerful arched nose, the disdainful mouth. It was a handsome face, arrogant, prideful, sure of self.

As he drew nearer, the rider slowed his big black to a walk. He reined in, his mount at a slant, all but blocking the trail. The cold eyes flickered from Kells to Hatfield, looked him up and down. Kells pulled up and so did Hatfield, within arm's length of the newcomer, who apparently dismissed him from his mind and centered his attention on Kells.

"So yuh're bringin' in double-holster men to do your work for yuh, Kells?" he remarked in tones that dripped contempt.

Kells flushed slightly, but when he spoke his voice was quiet.

"I notice you pack two guns, Cowdry," he remarked.

"But I don't use 'em to shoot folks in the back!" Cowdry blazed.

Kells' hand flashed to his holster. But Cowdry's draw was like the flicker of a sunbeam on a wave crest. Jim Hatfield, lunging forward, caught his wrist in the split second of time vouchsafed him, jerking it up with a sideways wrench that spun the gun from Cowdry's hand. Cowdry instantly drew with his left, but again Hatfield was there first. And this time the Lone Wolf meant business. Cowdry screamed in agony as his wrist bones were ground together as by the jaws of an iron vice. Sweat popped out on his face, sickly white under the tan. The second gun dropped from his nerveless fingers.

"A — a little more and you'll break the left one!" he panted. "If yuh do — I'll — I'll kill you!"

"Would be considerable of a chore with both your arms in good shape," Hatfield told him, easing his grip a trifle. "Behave if I turn you loose?"

"Y-yes, damn yuh!" Cowdry gasped. "Let go!"

Hatfield released him. Cowdry glared, his face twisted with rage, and nursed his aching wrists.

"I don't know what this is all about," Hatfield said, "but I never saw a shorthorn killing do anything much good. And you spoke plumb out of turn, feller. Nobody brought me in here, and nobody's moving me out till I'm ready to trail my rope. And any gun slinging I do will be on my own account. Ready to go, Kells?"

Wordless, Kells moved his horse forward in unison with Hatfield's. The Lone Wolf did not look back, but Kells did.

"Don't think for a minute *he* ain't plumb

capable of shootin' in the back," he warned grimly.

"He won't do much gun pointing for a few minutes yet," Hatfield replied confidently.

Kells shook his head. "Reckon yuh're right," he agreed. "Feller, I'd sure hate to have you get your hands around my neck!"

Hatfield smiled slightly, and changed the subject.

"What was the feller on the prod for?" he asked.

"He believes I killed his uncle, Walt Cowdry," Kells replied, adding bitterly, "and so do a lot more folks, I reckon. Yuh see, Walt Cowdry and me had some trouble. Last week Walt Cowdry was killed, as I told yuh last night. Found shot in the back in the mouth of Moon Valley. Nobody accused me of doin' him in, but I know what folks are thinkin'. Young Bern Cowdry has done considerable talkin', I know, but I let it pass till today. This was the first time he ever braced me to my face. Reckon I'd have got mine today if you hadn't been along. He's plumb pizen with a gun and mean as a teased snake."

" 'Peared a trifle ringey," Hatfield admitted. What he did not mention to Kells was that, to all appearances, Cowdry had deliberately tried to taunt the older man into reaching.

"And he knew Kells wouldn't have a chance," Hatfield told himself. "Say, this is a nice section, all right!"

For some minutes they rode in silence. When Hatfield finally spoke, his voice was casual.

"What did you and Walt Cowdry have trouble over?" he asked.

Kells seemed to hesitate, shooting a sideways glance at the Ranger.

"Tell yuh about that later," he replied.

Hatfield nodded and did not pursue the subject. He felt that Kells would talk when he was ready, not before.

A little later they rounded a bend and Kells pointed ahead.

"There's Moon Valley," he said.

From the slantwise view of it, Hatfield could see that the valley was really but a wide canyon walled by high cliffs. It appeared to be pretty heavily brush grown. In fact, nothing much could be made of the valley because of the stand of tall chaparral choking its mouth.

Another half mile and a broad and well travelled trail showed through the chaparral. They turned into this trail and Hatfield heard a familiar grinding, rumbling sound.

"What in blazes?" he exclaimed. "A stamp mill!"

"That's right," Kells replied. "I stamp my own ore."

They rode swiftly up the trail. Suddenly the chaparral belt ended and the broad expanse of Moon Valley lay before them.

The canyon was excellently grass grown for as far as Hatfield could see. It was dotted with groves and bristles of growth. There were plenty of cows in sight. A stream of water ran down one side. The canyon appeared to box at a distance of perhaps ten miles to the north.

"A good looking range," he remarked to Kells. "And you 'pear to be doing plenty of other business, too."

A few hundred yards ahead near the west wall of the canyon was the stamp mill. The air vibrated to the rumble of the huge steel pestles doing their ceaseless dance that ground the ore into a watery paste from which the precious metal would be extracted by the amalgam process.

The mill was not large, but the building that housed it was well constructed and new. Hatfield could see the arch of the mine tunnel that pierced the canyon wall, from which a cart laden with ore was just appearing.

Some distance beyond the mill was a ranchhouse, evidently much older than the mine buildings. It was set in a grove of burr oaks and the barn and corral and a few smaller buildings were in good repair.

"Yes, this is the Tumbling K, and over there," said Kells, "is the reason for my row with Walt Cowdry."

Hatfield stared. Kells had gestured toward neither mine, mill nor ranchhouse. He was pointing to a complacent looking black pig rooting around at the edge of the chaparral.

5

"Yes," Kells chuckled, "that darn old boar is to blame for everything. But I'll start at the beginning.

"Walt Cowdry owned just about all of this section, from over here on east and around to the north where the hills peter out. He held a heap more land than he had any use for. So when I came back to this country and wanted to set up in business for myself he sold me Moon Valley at a very reasonable price, and enough cows to start up with. That was about a year back.

"Well, I like pork chops, and right after I moved in and got going, I bought that boar and a few sows and turned 'em loose here to make out on the mesquite beans and so forth."

Hatfield nodded. "I see," he remarked, beginning to get the drift of what was coming.

"Uh-huh," Kells continued. "Less than

two weeks later, it happened. Last night you told me you know something about mining. Well, then yuh know that hogs are plumb good pocket miners. They root around the bushes and turn up little piles of dirt. Then along comes a rain and washes the piles down and exposes the gold, if there happens to be any around, sometimes right over a pocket. Well, that's just what happened. That old curly tail rooted up a pile over not far from the cliff face. A rain came and washed the dirt down and exposed a nice hunk of gold bearin' quartz. I'd had some experience with minin' over in California while I was wandering around, and I knew right off that hunk wasn't glacier drift or water float. I knew it had been busted loose from a parent body, perhaps by a stroke of lightnin' or by cracking brought about by frost and thaws. Anyhow, there it was."

"So you started hunting for the source," Hatfield interpolated.

"That's right," admitted Kells. "I started huntin'. The logical place to look, of course, was the cliff face. The vein was there. Not strange that it had never been hit on before. There must have been a tremendous upheaval here, millions of years back, and those cliffs were thrust up. There are two distinct rock formations. The outer one is not gold bearing quartz. The second layer is quartz. Somehow or other a section of the outer rock sluffed off, a very narrow section. I'd say freezing water seepin' into the cracks durin' the years was the cause. Anyhow, back in that narrow cleft was the outcroppin' of the vein. Nacherly I did some careful investigatin'. I decided the vein was worth working. It was. It ain't any Mother Lode, but I've been gettin' metal in payin' quantities. I figger if I knew more about the business, I'd do a heap better. I borrowed money on the spread and on the prospective output of the mine, built the stamp mill and went to work. I'll admit I'm runnin' pretty close to the ragged edge, and if I can't do a mite better, I may have trouble when my notes fall due, but I was always purty good on takin' chances — that's how I got my stake to buy the spread, poker winnin's and so on."

"A nice layout, anyhow," Hatfield said.

Kells nodded. "And I'd hate to lose it," he said. "But to come to Walt Cowdry. When Cowdry heard about my gold strike, he pawed sod for fair. Yuh see, that darn pig twirled his loop right after I moved in. I hadn't been here even a month. Cowdry right off accused me of knowin' the gold ledge was there all the time, and flim-flammin' him out of a valuable property. I couldn't convince him any different. I privately offered to cut him in on the mine — equal shares — but he was the sort that wouldn't listen to anything when he got on the prod. Called me about everything he could lay his hand to. I took it, 'cause I knew he felt he was right. He never got over it. Got worse as time went on, in fact. About ten days ago he met me in town, cut loose for fair and actually pulled his gun on me. I turned my back on him and walked away, with him yellin' at me to stand and fight and swearin' he'd get me sooner or later."

Kells paused to roll and light a cigarette, his eyes somber.

"Then," he concluded, "two days after our ruckus in town, Walt Cowdry's body was found right out there at the mouth of Moon Valley. He'd been shot in the back."

Jim Hatfield nodded thoughtfully. "Sort of put you on a spot," he agreed. "Did Cowdry have any enemies?"

"Not that anybody appeared to know about," Kells admitted. "Of course, there's Roma's Raiders. They've been raisin' hell and shovin' a chunk under the corner in this section for the past eight or nine months. Sheriff Walsh brought that up, and

I've a notion quite a few other folks agreed with him. But there are plenty of others who are mighty suspicious of me. It's even been talked some that I might be Roma hisself. Nobody knows for sure what he looks like, and he started operatin' not so long after I came back here. Yuh know how that sort of talk builds up. Young Bern Cowdry is plumb certain I did in his uncle and says so."

"Did Bern Cowdry inherit his uncle's property?" Hatfield asked.

Kells shook his head. "Nope," he replied. "Walt Cowdry left a daughter, and nacherly she came into everything. Bern's father was Walt Cowdry's older brother by a couple of years. He got killed in Arizona a little less than a year ago. That's how young Bern came to live with his uncle."

Kells' momentary hesitation when speaking of Walt Cowdry's brother's death was not lost on Hatfield. He wondered why, but did not comment or question at the moment.

"And now," continued Kells, "comes what I wanted to talk to you about. Yuh say yuh know somethin' about minin'?"

Hatfield nodded.

"Much?" Kells persisted.

"Considerable," Hatfield conceded. He did not see fit, at the moment, to tell Kells that before he joined up with the Rangers he had had three years in a famous college of engineering, that he had never lost interest in the subject and in the years that followed had kept up his studies, more than once putting his knowledge to good use in the course of his Ranger activities.

"I know mighty little about it," Kells admitted. "I worked around mines in California and got the hang of how it was done, but when it comes to real knowledge of the business, I just ain't there. I can't help but feel that if I knowed more, the mine would be doin' better. It did quite well at first, but of late it hasn't been doin' near so well. I can't figger it, but I also can't figger what to do about it. What I want to ask you is will yuh take over here and run things for me. I'll pay yuh considerable more than a chore of ridin' will. I know what that is, and a feller never gets very far at forty-per and found. I got my start after I got away from a rope and brandin' iron. What do yuh say?"

Hatfield did not speak for a moment. "Suppose we look things over first," he suggested. "Then I'll talk to you, tell you what I think."

"Fine!" exclaimed Kells. "We'll do that before we eat, if it's okay with you." He called a wrangler to take care of the horses.

First they gave the stamp mill a once-over. Hatfield decided it was a good two-stamp mill with a capacity sufficient to handle the output of the mine, at least for the present. The mill workers seemed to know their business. They regarded Hatfield curiously and the Lone Wolf noted that there was a drawing together of heads in low-voiced conversation after he passed a group.

The engine room and the boiler that provided power for the steam drills also proved satisfactory. Then they provided themselves with cap lights and entered the mine tunnel.

As they progressed along the bore, Hatfield examined the side walls minutely and with interest. As he did so, his black brows drew together until the concentration furrow was deep between them, a sure sign that the Lone Wolf was doing some hard thinking.

Finally they reached the end of the bore where the drills chattered, sledges thudded and the scrap of loading shovels echoed from the walls. A number of drill men and other workers were busy there.

Hatfield examined the cutting without comment, watched the progress of the drilling for a while, selected specimens of the ore being brought down and scrutinized them intently.

As in the mill, he noticed a drawing together of heads and low voiced observations.

"Let's go eat," he abruptly said to Kells. "I'll talk with you outside."

At the comfortably furnished ranchhouse, an old Mexican cook set a good meal before them. Kells talked about the ranch and the mine, but Hatfield was mostly silent, apparently deep in thought. After they had finished eating, they adjourned to the living room of the *casa* for a smoke.

"Well?" Kells asked at length. "What do yuh say? Goin' to tie up with me?"

Hatfield let the full force of his long green eyes rest on the other's face for a moment.

"Yes," he said, "under a condition."

"What's that?"

"Under the condition that I am in full charge, absolutely and without reservation, to do whatever I see fit, to issue any orders I feel are necessary. If you countermand one order I give, I'm through."

Kells stared at him, slightly bewildered. The steady green eyes did not waver. The mine owner instinctively realized that Hatfield meant just what he said, no more, no less. He also sensed a rising conviction within himself that this tall, level-eyed cowboy knew what he was talking about.

"Done!" he exclaimed. "From now on, everybody is takin' orders from you, includin' myself.

"Funny," he added with a chuckle, "I ain't knowed yuh twenty-four hours, and here I am puttin' my whole business in your hands. Yuh're a strange sort of feller, Hatfield. I felt that last night when Sheriff Walsh took to yuh like he did. Walsh don't usually like anybody over much, or anything else he can't eat. I've a notion most everybody yuh meet takes to yuh."

"Not quite," Hatfield smiled. "All right, let's go."

He stood up, hitched his cartridge belts a trifle higher. His face had suddenly set in bleak lines and Kells noticed that his strangely colored eyes had changed. No longer were they the green of a summer sea under sunny skies. Now they were the color of that same sea under winter's lowering storm clouds, a cold and smoky gray. Kells abruptly felt funny along his backbone, he couldn't say why.

"The mine first," Hatfield said as they left the house. "We'll stop at the mill later."

With long, lithe strides he led the way along the tunnel, standing aside from time to time to let mule carts laden with ore rumble past. They reached the head of the bore. Kells' shout called the workers from their tasks.

"Boys," he said, "this is Mr. Hatfield. He's in charge here from now on, absolutely. Whatever he says goes."

Hatfield gazed at the ring of curious faces for a moment.

"Who's in charge of the drillers here?" he asked abruptly.

A big hulking man with an enormous spread of shoulders and long, hairy arms stepped forward. He had bristling red hair, truculent dark eyes, and a stubble of reddish beard.

"I'm running things here," he growled in surly tones.

"That so?" Hatfield asked. "Well, just what is the notion of making the cut partly through the casing rock — rock that has about as much metal content as a grindstone?"

The big fellow glared. "You tryin' to tell me my business?" he rumbled menacingly.

"Exactly," Hatfield replied. "Either you don't know your business, or you're deliberately pulling something. Which is it — ignorance or slick-ironing?"

The driller boss flushed scarlet. His hair seemed to bristle. His eyes glared. With a roar of rage he rushed, his huge fists swinging.

Hatfield hit him, left and right. He went down as if pole-axed. With another yell he bounded to his feet, blood spurting from his cut lips. Again he rushed, striking out with terrific force.

Hatfield weaved aside, and hit him again with both hands. Again he went down, gasping and floundering.

But he could take it. He scrambled to his feet, a trifle more slowly this time, and again he rushed. Hatfield side-stepped, but his foot came down on a fragment of rock and for an instant he staggered, half off balance. The big man's fist found its mark, thudding against the Ranger's jaw. Hatfield reeled back against the side wall and with a yell of triumph, the driller rushed in for the kill.

He met a straight right that stopped him in mid-stride. As he sagged on his feet, Hatfield's left lashed out with every ounce of his two hundred pounds of bone and muscle behind it. The smack against the driller's jaw was like that of a butcher's cleaver on a side of meat.

The big fellow seemed to take unto himself wings. He flew through the air, great limbs revolving, landed on his back and stayed there. Hatfield rubbed his tingling knuckles and spoke, his voice quiet and unhurried.

"Pack him outside and throw a bucket of water over him," he directed. "When he gets his senses back, tell him not to be around when I come out or he'll get a real working over. Now who is there here that's capable of taking charge of the drilling?"

There was a moment of hesitation, then a wizened little old fellow stepped forward. His faded blue eyes met Hatfield's without flinching.

"Reckon I can do it," he said, "so long as I'm workin' for somebody who knows what he's doin' and gives straight orders. My name's Tom Barnes."

"Okay, Barnes," Hatfield instantly replied. "You're in charge of the work here." He turned to Kells.

"What were you paying that horned toad they're packing out?" he asked.

Kells named the sum.

Hatfield nodded. "Barnes gets ten dollars more per," he said. "All right, Barnes, how would you change the cutting from here on?"

The old man reacted without hesitation, making his suggestions precisely and to the point. Hatfield nodded with satisfaction.

"I won't need to tell you much," he said.

"Okay, Mr. Barnes, get your drills going. I'll check with you tomorrow. Come on, Kells, let's look the mill over again. We're not needed here."

As they headed down the tunnel, the bewildered owner turned to Hatfield.

"What in blazes is it all about?" he demanded.

"I don't know," Hatfield replied grimly. "For some reason or other, that head driller was veering the cutting away from the lode. Half the rock they were bringing down was absolutely worthless."

"But wouldn't the others know that?" Kells asked.

"Not necessarily," Hatfield replied. "They are drillers and laborers, not miners in the real sense of the word. I'm pretty sure that old feller, Barnes, had caught on from the way he answered me. And I think the mill men were puzzled about the kind of rock they were getting for the stamps. But the casing and the gangue — the metal bearing rock — is almost identical in appearance and this is, comparatively speaking, low-grade ore that does not have an outstanding metal veining or flecking. I'd give most of the workers the benefit of the doubt. Barnes, I'm pretty sure, caught on, as I said, but figured it was best for

71

him to keep his mouth shut. You can't blame him. That head driller was a pretty salty proposition."

"I know all the men were scairt of him," Kells agreed. "But you handled him like he was a scrub calf."

"He was awkward on his feet and lost his temper," Hatfield deprecated. "Glad he didn't get his arms around me."

"Uh-huh," Kells remarked dryly, "so am I. You and me might have been explainin' a killin' to Sheriff Walsh. I ain't forgot what yuh did to Bern Cowdry when yuh took hold of him. And Bern ain't no push-over for anybody.

"But why in blazes was Purdy, the head driller, doin' what he was?" Kells demanded in perplexity.

Hatfield shrugged. "For some reason he wanted to cut your production down," he replied. "What that reason was and what was back of it are something else again. I've a notion your next mill clean-up will show quite a rise in metal."

Just then they met the four returning laborers who had been assigned the chore of packing Purdy's unconscious form to the outside.

"He come to before we made it to the tunnel mouth," one of them explained. "He cussed somethin' awful, but he kept on goin'."

"Reckon he's headed down the valley by now," Kells chuckled. "He kept a horse in the barn and rode to town most every night. The other men sleep and eat in a bunkhouse I built for 'em back of the *casa*. They usually stay here at night except on paydays. Then I have 'em druv over to Sanders for a bust. They all seem to be purty good men."

Hatfield nodded, but reserved decision. He strongly suspected that at least one of the mill workers was in cahoots with Purdy.

Hatfield spent the remainder of the day going over assay reports, production sheets and other details with Kells.

"I don't see any reason why you won't be doing as well from now on as you did the first few months of operations," he told the owner. "You evidently showed a fair profit on your investment at first, but of late I'd say you haven't done much more than break even."

"That's right," Kells agreed.

Hatfield pondered a moment.

"Anybody tried to buy you out here?" he asked suddenly.

"Why, no," Kells replied. "Reckon everybody hereabouts knows I wouldn't sell. Everybody knows I'm most interested in makin' Moon Valley a payin' cow ranch and makin' a home of the place. If the mine should fail up tomorrow, I wouldn't be pertickler bothered, so long as I could hold on to the spread."

"But suppose the mine did peter out and you couldn't meet your notes or even the interest?" Hatfield asked.

"Well," said Kells, "in that case, I reckon the bank at Sanders would find itself in the cow business."

"I see," Hatfield nodded thoughtfully.

Hatfield was even more thoughtful as he sat in his room in the ranchhouse that night before going to bed.

"It's like everything else that's been happening since I landed in this section," he declared. "It just doesn't make sense. From all appearances somebody hired that slick-iron Purdy to cut production at the mine. It was being done in a smart way, too. He could have veered the cutting still more and left the vein altogether. But that was liable to cause somebody to get suspicious. Kells, or the bank, which has an interest in the success or failure of the mine, might have hired a mining engineer to try and relocate the lost vein. And then the jig would have been up. But a slow and steady decrease in production is something else again. It is a logical occurrence in workings like this one. Would indicate a gradual petering out of the lode. That has happened in lots of places. They had a good chance to get away with it.

"But why? Why should anybody be so anxious to put Kells out of business? To get hold of the mine? There is where it doesn't make sense. The ore is low-grade ore, with little chance of ever being anything else. It will make Kells some money, but it won't make him rich. Why should anybody cook up a dangerous scheme like that, one that would send somebody to the penitentiary if the facts came to light, just to get control of such a property. No, it sure doesn't make sense, but there it is. And who is back of it? Purdy certainly wasn't acting on his own. He hasn't got that kind of brains. Just a stupid hired hand, the sort that's ready to doublecross anybody for small pay. Perhaps I'd have done better to have kept him on for a spell. Might have learned something."

He drew the tiny opal-eyed image from his pocket and studied it long and earnestly. The demoniac little face seemed to leer at him derisively.

"This thing is the key to the explanation or I'm a heap mistaken," he mused. "But what that can be, I've not the least notion.

Well, it doesn't much matter, anyhow. My business here now is to run down Roma's Raiders, whoever they may be."

The night was quite warm, so Hatfield put out the light and sat for a while beside the open window. He was thinking of turning in when his keen ears caught the sound of stealthy footsteps on the ground below. He leaned forward, peering into the darkness. A moment later he was almost sure he saw a shadowy figure cross the open space between the ranchhouse and the mill.

The figure did not reappear, however, and there was no further sound. After some minutes of watching and listening, Hatfield was about to dismiss the whole occurrence as a figment of his imagination. But as he turned from the window to prepare for bed, he saw a flicker of light in the direction of the mill. It reappeared, stronger and brighter, and abruptly became a reddish glow rising and spreading.

An instant later, Hatfield was pounding down the stairs, roaring *"fire"* at the top of his voice.

6

Alarmed shouts sounded from the workers' quarters in the rear of the ranchhouse. Answering yells came from the bunkhouse by the corral. Men came pouring forth in all stages of undress.

"Water!" Hatfield thundered at them. "The mill's a-fire."

He led the rush to the building, crashed open the door and leaped inside.

The fire was burning briskly in a far corner, crackling the oil soaked floor boards, leaping up the tinder-dry wall.

With buckets, tubs and anything that came to hand, the workers attacked the flames. A line was formed to the nearby creek and the containers passed from hand to hand.

Hatfield and Kells and two of the cowhands fought the flames with the water the bucket line passed them in a continuous stream of containers, sloshing it against the burning wall, stamping out the spreading smoulders on the floor.

For minutes it was touch and go, for a brisk wind blowing up the valley fanned the fire and sent it leaping and roaring toward the roof.

Gradually, however, they got the flames under control. The whole end wall of the mill was blackened and blistered by the time the last glowing ember was drowned out.

"How did yuh come to spot it, Hatfield?" Kells asked, wiping his grimy face.

"Just good luck," the Ranger replied. "Was standing by the open window and just getting ready to go to bed when I saw it flicker up."

"Well, if yuh hadn't, we would have lost the mill," Kells declared with conviction. "If she'd gotten just a mite more of a start there would have been no stoppin' it, with this wind blowin'. Much obliged, feller."

"Don't thank me," Hatfield chuckled. "Think I want to find myself out of a job?"

Kells glanced around, to insure that there was no spark still smouldering.

"Reckon some careless jigger dropped a burnin' cigarette," he growled. "If these fellers had ever got caught in a grass fire out on the range, they'd be more careful how they throw butts around."

Hatfield said nothing, but he had his own very definite opinion as to how the fire started.

The following morning, the identity of the mysterious night prowler Hatfield saw was pretty well established. Also, Hatfield's suspicion that Purdy must have had a sidekick in the mill working with him was confirmed.

"Shelton, the foreman, ain't here this mornin'," a mill hand informed Kells. "He must have slid out durin' the night. His bed wasn't slept in."

Hatfield was not particularly surprised.

"Purdy couldn't very well have gotten by with what he was doing unless he had somebody working with him in the mill," he told Kells. "And it was sort of logical to think that somebody would be the mill foreman. I didn't say anything to you yesterday, because I didn't want to chance casting suspicion on a jigger who might be plumb innocent."

Briefly, he told Kells of what he had seen and heard from the window of his room just before he spotted the fire.

"That was Shelton, all right," he concluded. "The sidewinder made a last try to make trouble before he trailed his rope."

"Yuh figger he started the fire?"

"Of course, who else! I knew last night it had been deliberately set. The minute I busted into the mill I smelt burning oil. The whole floor and wall in that corner was drenched with it. Check up and you'll find a couple of containers are missing."

Kells swore viciously. "I'd sure like to line sights with that hellion," he concluded. "But why did he do it? To get even for us firin' Purdy?"

"He would have put you on a bad spot, right now, if the mill had been destroyed," Hatfield remarked. "Somebody is trying mighty hard to put you out of business, Kells."

"But why?" asked the bewildered owner.

"That's what I would like to know," Hatfield replied. "But it sure looks like somebody is almighty anxious to have you fail. Got any bad enemies that you know of?"

Kells shook his head. "Not unless yuh'd call Bern Cowdry an enemy," he replied. "Cowdry ain't got no use for me, but he don't strike me as the sort that would do a thing like settin' fire to the mill to even up."

Hatfield had already formed a like opinion.

"Was Cowdry unfriendly to you before his uncle got cashed in?" he asked.

"No," Kells replied positively. "We weren't

friends, but there was never any hard feelings before Walt Cowdry was drygulched. Bern was always civil enough when we happened to meet, which wasn't over often."

"That would appear to let Bern Cowdry out of it," Hatfield said. "For Purdy had been pulling his stunt for the past three months or so. The production sheets show that plainly."

Several busy days followed. First of all, Hatfield gave careful attention to the stamp mill and its employees. The operation of resolving the gold from the ore was a tedious and intricate process. Two tall, upright rods of iron as large as a man's ankle, and heavily shod with a mass of steel and iron at their lower ends, were framed together like a gate. These rods rose and fell, one after the other, in a ponderous dance in an iron box called a battery. Each stamp weighed six hundred pounds.

The ore was shovelled into the battery and the ceaseless dance of the stamps pulverized the rock to powder. A stream of water that trickled into the battery turned it into a creamy paste. The minute particles were driven through a fine wire screen that fitted close around the battery, and were washed into great tubs warmed by super-heated steam. These were the amalgamating pans.

The mass of pulp in the pans was kept constantly stirred by revolving mullers. A quantity of quicksilver was always kept in the battery and this seized some of the liberated particles of gold and held onto them. Quicksilver was also shaken in a fine shower into the pans about every half hour through a buckskin sack. Quantities of coarse salt and sulphate of copper were added from time to time to assist in the amalgamation by destroying base metals which coated the gold and would not let it unite with the quicksilver.

Streams of muddy water flowed always from the pans and were carried off in broad wooden troughs to the outside. Atoms of gold floated on the top of the water. Coarse blankets were laid in the troughs to catch them and little riffles charged with quicksilver were placed here and there across the troughs also. The riffles had to be cleaned and the blankets washed out every evening to get the accumulations of metal.

Many times during the day a little of the pulp was scooped from the pans and washed in a horn spoon till nothing was left in the spoon but some little dull globules of quicksilver in the bottom. If they were too soft and yielding, salt of sulphate of copper was added to the pan. If the globules were crisp to the touch and would retain a dint, they had collected all the gold they could seize and hold. This meant that the pans needed a fresh charge of quicksilver.

At the end of the week the machinery was stopped for the clean-up. The pulp was taken from the pans and batteries and the mud and other rubbish washed away. The accumulated mass of quicksilver with its imprisoned gold was molded into heavy, compact balls. Then the balls were placed in an iron retort that had a pipe leading from it to a container of water. A roasting heat was applied to the retort. The quicksilver turned to vapor, escaped through the pipe into the container and the water turned the vapor back into quicksilver once more which could be used over in the process of amalgamation.

The retort was opened and the lump of practically pure gold was taken out. This was melted up and made into a brick by pouring it into an iron mold.

All these intricacies required careful supervision and each was vulnerable to sabotage of one sort or another.

But before two days had passed, Hatfield was satisfied that no more of the workers in the mill had been implicated in the plot.

"Us fellers had a mighty good notion

something was going on," the stamp man he elevated to the position of foreman confided. "We knew we were gettin' rock for the batteries that had no business there. But Purdy and Shelton were cold propositions to go up against. So we just decided to lay low and hope that things would work out. And they did."

The work in the mine was also progressing satisfactorily. Old Tom Barnes proved capable and trustworthy and in possession of a fund of mining lore that steadily improved production.

"A straight cut ain't the thing for this lode," he told Hatfield. "She's a zig-zag vein. So I figger to make lateral cuts along with the main bore, if it's okay with you."

"Go to it," Hatfield told him. "I see you know your business. I'll check with you from time to time, and I'll try and improve the ventilating system. Those lateral cuts will be hot and dusty if we don't take care of them. We don't want any accidents."

"We won't have any," Barnes declared. "I'm keepin' a close eye on everything that goes on."

"There'll be bonuses for increased production," Hatfield promised. "You can pass the word along."

Barnes departed to take care of the chore,

grinning with pleasure.

Hatfield decided on a trip to town to arrange for equipment needed to install the improved ventilation system he had promised Barnes, the head driller.

"You handle it," Kells told him. "You know all about it and I don't. Hutchinson's general store will place the order for yuh and make delivery."

Hatfield reached Sanders without incident. After completing his business at the general store, he dropped in on Sheriff Walsh for a visit. He found the sheriff in a very bad temper.

"The Bar B lost a hundred cows night before last," Walsh explained. "Old Man Brady is fit to be hogtied. This is gettin' serious, Hatfield. This is cow country, minin' is just a side line, and a thing like this can plumb ruin the section if it keeps up. We ain't got any big spreads hereabouts and the boys can't stand such losses. It'll mean goin' out of business for them if it ain't stopped."

"Where did they go?" Hatfield asked.

"South to the River and across," replied the sheriff. "There's a prime market for wet cows the other side of the Rio Grande right now. I trailed 'em to the river, but they had too much of a start."

"And you figure the outfit you call Roma's Raiders is responsible?"

"Of course," growled the sheriff. "Who else?"

"How did they get to be called Roma's Raiders?" Hatfield asked. "Sort of an unusual sounding name."

"A few years back there was a Mexican owlhoot named Roma who kicked up a lot of hell hereabouts," said the sheriff. "But the Rangers killed him and busted up his outfit. When this new bunch started operatin', somebody said it must be Roma's Raiders back, and the name stuck, that's all."

"And now everything is Roma's Raiders," Hatfield remarked thoughtfully. "No matter what happens, Roma's Raiders get blamed for it, even though the chores may be pulled by other gangs snukin' in to take advantage of opportunity. Something happens and folks say 'Roma's Raiders,' which makes it easier for the other bunches and harder for the peace officer."

"Reckon yuh're right there," agreed the sheriff. "Did yuh tie onto a job with Kells?"

Hatfield explained the work he was doing for Kells.

"Glad to hear it," said the sheriff. "Kells is a first-rate cowman, but I figger he don't know over much about minin'. He needs somebody who does know to handle things for him. I always liked Kells, no matter what folks have been sayin' about him of late."

"You don't think he had anything to do with Walt Cowdry's death, then?" Hatfield asked.

"Hell, no," Walsh replied. "Kells ain't the sort to go shootin' in the back, I'll bet my last peso on that. He's purty handy with a gun, and he ain't got any yaller around his backbone. He took a heap from Walt Cowdry, but there's a good reason for that as I reckon yuh'll find out sooner or later."

The sheriff apparently did not see fit to elaborate on the "reason" for the moment and Hatfield refrained from questions.

Hatfield asked the sheriff if he could recommend a mill hand and a driller, casually mentioning that Purdy and Shelton had left Kells' employ.

"Reckon I can find yuh a couple of rock busters," Walsh admitted. "There's usually one or two hangin' around. Them hardrock men quit jobs whenever the notion strikes 'em, and take up with some other outfit. I remember Purdy. A first-rate rock man but a hard proposition. He was in quite a few ruckuses here in town until I threatened to throw him in the calaboose for a spell. Then he cooled down a mite. He used to play poker a lot with young Bern Cowdry and a few other jiggers. 'Peared to be a purty good card player. Usually won. Cowdry most always loses, but stays hopeful. I don't recall much about Shelton. Reckon he might have been one of the poker players if he happened to be a sidekick of Purdy's, which I reckon he was, seein' that they quit together. Nope, I ain't seen either of 'em durin' the past few days."

Hatfield thanked the sheriff and departed to the Ace-Full for a bite to eat before riding back to the Tumbling K.

As he pushed through the swinging doors, his glance fell on young Bern Cowdry sitting at a nearby table where a poker game was in progress. Cowdry's face was flushed, his eyes glowing. His hands twitched as he manipulated the cards.

"A gambling man," Hatfield mused, "the sort that goes for cards like some folks go for red-eye. A regular passion with him, I'd say. And that sort usually loses. Too impatient and reckless. Have to be in every pot, no matter what kind of a hand they hold."

Cowdry glanced up at that moment and met the Ranger's eyes. His face tightened, his hands tensed, the fingers spreading out claw-like on the green cloth.

Hatfield stood perfectly still, waiting.

But Cowdry apparently thought better of anything he had in mind. With a swift glare, he dropped his eyes to the cards again and went on playing as if nothing had happened. Hatfield walked to the lunch counter and placed his order.

He caught a glint of Cowdry's eyes in his direction as he left the saloon a little later. But the young cowman did not rise from the table or make any other overt move.

Hatfield rode back to the Tumbling K very thoughtful and very watchful.

7

Several days later, Kells announced his intention of riding to town. Certain supplies needed to be replenished and he wished to draw money from the bank to fill the pay envelopes that would be distributed the next day. He asked Hatfield to accompany him.

As they rode to town, Kells talked about matters pertaining to the mine and the ranch, but Hatfield was mostly silent, giving careful attention to the terrain over which they rode. No movement of twig or branch escaped observation. He studied the actions of birds on the wing and of little animals in the brush. His gaze constantly roved over the thickets and hillsides. He did not expect trouble, but he was taking no chances. Too many sinister happenings had taken place since his arrival in the section.

"Sanders will howl tomorrow," Kells chuckled. "It's payday for all the mines.

Most of the spreads pay off, too, so everybody can take part in the bust. Sheriff Walsh won't even have time to eat and the temper he'll be in! Interfere with Tom's eatin' and he ain't fit to live with."

As they entered the main street, they saw a buckboard standing beside the railroad station. On the seat was a girl. Hatfield noticed that as Kells' eyes rested on her, he flushed and grew ill at ease.

The girl spotted them immediately and waved a little sun-golden hand.

"Come on over, Hugh," she called.

Hesitantly, Kells turned his horse. He and Hatfield dismounted beside the buckboard. The girl leaped lightly to the ground to greet them.

"Mary, this is Jim Hatfield, my new mine engineer, and a mighty good friend," Kells introduced. "Jim, this is Mary Cowdry."

Mary Cowdry was not very big, except for her eyes, which were astonishingly so and a deep violet-blue in color. She had a sweetly formed red mouth, a slightly tip-tilted little nose with a freckle or two delicately powdering the bridge. There was a wholesome outdoor look about her and her smile was engaging. But there was a somber shadow in the blue eyes that Hatfield felt did not belong there. She shook hands frankly and smiled up at him.

And when she looked at Kells, and Kells returned the look, a number of things that had been puzzling Hatfield were abruptly made plain, among them Kells' reluctance to tangle with old Walt Cowdry, the girl's father.

"I haven't seen you for ages, Hugh," she said reproachfully.

Kells flushed miserably. "Mary," he replied, "you know what folks have been sayin'," he muttered.

"Yes, I know," the girl replied, "but nobody could make me believe for a moment that you had anything to do with — with Dad's death. You know me better than that, Hugh. At least you ought to."

"But then there's Bern," Kells pointed out. "He's on the prod against me for fair."

Mary Cowdry's round little white chin suddenly tilted upward and in a very firm fashion.

"I hate to have to say it, but I own the Cross C now, and I have all the say as to what is done and what isn't," she replied. "If Bern doesn't like my — my friends, he can go back to Arizona. Oh, he's a good cowman, all right, and has been a lot of help to me and has been most kind and considerate since — since what happened. But he needn't think he's telling me what to do or deciding with whom I shall associate."

"It makes me feel a heap better to hear yuh say that, Mary," Kells said gratefully, "but I don't want to make trouble for you. You've had enough as it is. Why are yuh in town?"

"I'm here to meet a cook who is supposed to arrive on the noon train," the girl replied. "Charley Lake of the Bradded L over by Rio has two fine Chinese working in his kitchen. He doesn't really need but one, so he's leting me have the other. The first of last week, old Miguel left. You remember Miguel, the Mexican Bern brought up from Angelo. He was a good cook, but for some reason or other he cleared out all of a sudden without giving notice or saying a word to anybody. He just left. Bern rode around to every place he thought he might be but couldn't find a sign of him. Stuffy Jones took over the kitchen and has nearly poisoned all of us. I had to take over myself. The boys were all threatening to quit."

"Stuffy has notions when it comes to cookin'," Kells chuckled.

"He certaintly has — *some* notions," the girl replied disgustedly. "Sauerkraut cooked in coffee! That was the last straw."

"No idea why Miguel took a notion to

trail his twine?"

"None at all," Mary answered. "He just left. I can't understand it. He always seemed perfectly contented."

Jim Hatfield suddenly played a hunch.

"Ma'am," he said, "what sort of a looking jigger was Miguel? I met an old Mexican out on the desert on my way to this section. I've a notion he was headed for a long trip. Wonder if he could have been your cook?"

"Why, Miguel was an old man," the girl described. "A little wizened old man. Wasn't anything much to him but bones with skin stretched over them. Looked half starved all the time, though he seemed healthy enough. His hair was almost white."

"Sure just about fits the feller I saw," Hatfield replied gravely.

"Did he say where he was going?" the girl asked.

Hatfield shook his head. "Nope, he didn't say. Fact is, I've a notion he didn't really know himself."

"All men are that way," Mary Cowdry declared with the experience and conviction of twenty-one. "They just go riding off with nothing particular in mind, just to be going somewhere."

She shot a challenging glance at Kells as she spoke. The big fellow grinned a trifle sheepishly but apparently decided he was better off not to argue the point. He wisely changed the subject.

An hour later, Kells and Hatfield rode back to the Tumbling K, the former in a happier frame of mind than he had shown since Hatfield knew him.

An uneventful fortnight passed smoothly, with everything going well and the production of the mine steadily increasing. Old Tom Barnes proved to be an efficient mine superintendent and Hatfield was glad to find more and more time to ride the range with Kells and his small but able crew of cowhands, in the course of which he met and became acquainted with quite a few of the other spread owners and liked them.

The regard was mutual. "That big feller," declared crusty old man Brady of the Bar B, biggest and best ranch in the section, "that big feller has got more cow savvy than any two men I ever met. I'd sure like to get him away from Kells."

"You and quite a few others," grunted taciturn Mark Crane of the Lazy C. "But unless I'm a heap mistook, he ain't the sort to leave one boss without reason to sign up with another. But I'm glad he's around. We can use him come roundup time, and that ain't far off. He's the kind of a feller we been needin' around here for quite a spell."

Brady and others present nodded emphatic agreement.

Roma's Raiders were conspicuous for their absence on the scene, which made nobody sad.

"Maybe the hellion has gone back to Mexico or someplace," Kells hazarded hopefully.

"Not likely," Hatfield disagreed. "Just waiting his chance to line sights on something big." His eyes grew thoughtful as he spoke. "I wonder," he muttered.

"What say?" asked Kells.

"Just humming," the Lone Wolf parried. "You say roundup starts next week?"

"That's right," said Kells. "And we'll have a real holiday. Quit being miners for a spell and really get back to the cow business, which won't make either one of us feel bad."

Hatfield nodded. "When a jigger's born with horse-flesh and grass rope in his blood he never gets it out, no matter what he's turned his hand to," he replied.

"A week of peace and everybody getting along together," Kells continued.

Hatfield nodded again. It was true. The roundup is the life blood of the rangeland. During roundup, personal feuds go by the board and everybody works in harmony. A man who starts trouble during a roundup receives scant mercy from his fellows.

"There'll be a big trail herd to move," said Kells.

"You don't ship by train, then?"

"Not this year," Kells replied. "We used to. But now a Kansas City firm has built packing and processing houses over to Creston east of here, and they've contracted to take every head the section can get together to us fellers' advantage. It's a four-day drive, but it saves plenty in shipping charges."

"Drive's never been made before?"

"Nope," Kells answered. "This will be the first time."

"You familiar with the country over which the herd will trail?" Hatfield asked.

Kells shook his head. "And I don't guess anybody is," he said. "Oh, fellers around here have ridden to Creston some time or other, I guess, but just riding through a country isn't the same as running cows through it. You can't take short cuts with cows like you can with just a horse. But we'll make out."

Hatfield nodded and said no more.

"Meeting over to Brady's *casa* tonight to arrange roundup details," Kells remarked the next day. "We'll both go."

It was Brady himself who suggested Jim

Hatfield be made roundup and trail boss.

"He's got the savvy and a way of getting folks to do what he says," insisted the cantankerous Bar B owner. "And he's new to the section and ain't stocked up yet with likes and dislikes and such damn foolishness."

Suggestions from Brady were usually well received, and this one proved no exception. Other owners had already formed similar opinions concerning Jim Hatfield.

8

Brrrrrrrrrrr! Jangle-jangle-jangle! Brrrrrrr!

It was four o'clock in the morning and the cook's alarm clock had just let go. The clock had a raucous and penetrating voice and to make matters worse, the old hellion insisted on placing it on a tin pan turned bottom-side up and set on a rock. The racket was prodigious.

From the sleepy cowboys snugged in their blankets came groans and curses.

Brrrrrrrrrr!

The curses loudened. "Shut that blankety-blank thing off!" somebody bawled.

The cook reached out a languid arm to snap the lever. His hand struck the clock. It went over with a bang. The pan teetered, jostled, and clock and pan went clattering down the side of the rock.

More cursing followed.

"If I thought I wouldn't put a hole through the pan, I'd drill the blankety-blank dead center!" someone declared bitterly.

The cook crawled out of his blankets and put on his boots. He stumbled over to the mess-box and selected from one of its compartments a piece of rich pine from which he proceeded to whittle a handful of shavings. He scraped away the ashes that covered the fire hole, first carefully setting aside a huge coffee boiler. Upon the exposed bed of glowing coals he dropped the shavings. They caught almost instantly, flaring up in a bright flame. He dropped bits of wood on the growing fire, then larger chunks. The fire began to crackle and sputter. He hauled out his "wreck pan," a huge dishpan into which, upon finishing eating, gents dropped their dirty dishes. He reached for a cluster of tin cups; they slipped from his fingers and landed in the pan with a bang like the crack of doom.

"Oh, hell! what's the use!" growled a thoroughly aroused puncher as he crawled from his blankets. "Hey, you slab-sided horned toad, how about some coffee?"

"Come and get it," grunted the cook, reaching for the boiler.

The puncher tugged on his boots and headed for the fire. The cook poured him a steaming cupful. The cowboy squatted comfortably on his heels and regarded the cook gloomily over the rim of the cup.

"Why in blazes was cooks ever made, anyhow?" he complained peevishly and gulped the coffee.

The cook said something theological and refilled his cup. Still grumbling his opinion of cowhands in general and the one present in particular, he reached for a biscuit pan. It slipped from his hand and landed on the heavy iron top of a Dutch oven.

The whole round-up crew got up.

The cook was soon dishing up hot biscuits, delicious thin slabs of steak covered with crisp, brown batter, boiled rice and sorghum molasses. He removed the cover from a pickle keg, revealing a hole about three inches square cut in its top. He laid a long-handled fork across the hole, with which to spear out the pickle without which no cowhand could really enjoy a meal.

"Take 'em as they come," he warned all and sundry. "No fishin' around for little onions or cauliflowers. What you haul out with the first poke is what you eat."

Brady's Bar B spread, centrally located, had been designated as the main holding spot and here the collected cows were held in close herd. The troops of cowboys under the designated leaders rode out over the range. Soon these groups broke up and into small parties or single units until the hands were separated by distances that varied with the topography of the country.

Each man's duty was to hunt out all the cattle on the ground over which he rode, carefully searching for scattered individual animals or small bunches. These were gathered together and driven to the holding spot. As the herd grew, the riders changed horses and invaded the concentrated mass of cattle. The horses now were especially trained cutting horses and knew their business as well as did their riders. The cutting out would begin, calling for skillful and bold horsemanship and involving considerable personal danger.

The cows wanted were divorced from the main herd and driven before the tally man. Then, as indicated by their brands, they were distributed among the various subsidiary holding spots which were the individual corralling of the animals belonging to the ranches participating in the roundup.

Here again there was cutting. Cattle wanted for shipping were the beef cut. The culls and the cutbacks were allowed to roam once more. After being properly classified, they were driven to their home range and turned loose. The beef cut was held in close formation.

Calves were branded in accordance with the brand worn by their mothers. Out would flash a hissing rope. A startled bawl of the calf. The rope would hum taut as the trained horse took up the slack. The calf would be dragged to the fire where the various branding irons were heating. The rider would leather his way along the taut rope to the jumping, bawling calf.

"Bar B!" he would shout.

"Bar B!" the tally man would repeat, writing it down in his book.

The cowboy caught the calf under the flank and by the neck. Over it went with a bleat of terror. Another hand would run forward and grip a leg. The glowing iron came out of the fire. There was a crisping and sizzling, the acrid smell of scorched hair. A bawl from the calf, then another bawl as its ears were notched.

Off came the rope. The calf scrambled to its feet and bleated its way toward its anxious and angry mother who had been fended away from the scene of operations. The cow licked the wound and the calf quickly forgot all about its unpleasant experience.

With the instinct of the born cattleman, Jim Hatfield loved the roundup. The dust, the heat, the sweat, the shouting and the tumult of hectic activity. The day began at four in the morning. It ended when the lovely blue dusk sifted down like an impalpable dust from the surrounding hills.

In the blaze of the noonday sun, under the stars of night the work went on in one phase or another. In deference to the turbulent condition of the range, Hatfield refrained from night drives consisting of small squads of hands sent out ten or fifteen miles from the chuck-wagons to camp on their own hook and early in the morning begin driving cattle in the country designated for the next day's working.

"We'll hold 'em here where we can keep an eye on 'em after dark," he told the spread owners. There was no argument.

So after the sun had set and the moon soared up in the west, the only sounds of activity were the singing of the night hawks and the steady clump of their horses' irons as they rode ceaselessly around the bunched and sleeping cattle.

At last all was ready and the herd took the trail. The morning sunlight glinted from tossing horn points and smouldered on shaggy backs. From under the churning hoofs whose slow pound was as the thunder of the surf on a shingly shore, the dust rose in a golden cloud that quickly powdered man and beast. A mighty stream of moving flesh, the herd rolled on toward Creston.

Near the head of the herd rode the point men, guiding, directing. A third of the way back where the herd would begin to bend in a change of course were the swing riders. Another third back came the flank riders whose duty it was to aid the swing riders to block the cows from wandering sideways and to drive off any foreign cattle that tried to join the marching herd.

Bringing up the rear were the drag riders, cursing the dust and the slower or more obstinate animals. The drag, or tail, was the home of the incompetents, the footsore, the weary and the lazy, and a hospital for the ill and for chance infants born during the course of the drive. It was the most disagreeable post, but highly important.

Following the cattle came the remuda of spare horses in the charge of the wranglers. After them rumbled the chuck wagons driven by the cook and his helpers.

Nobody rode directly in front of the herd, but later in the day, Jim Hatfield, the range and trail boss, would scout far ahead and pick out a suitable bedding-down place for the night. And before evening the chuck wagon would also forge to the front so a meal would be ready for the hungry hands as soon as the chore of bedding down was finished.

The first day and night of the drive passed without incident. Hatfield pushed the herd hard the first day out. He desired to get the cows off their familiar home range as quickly as possible. Once upon new ground the tendency to stray was diminished. After the first day he planned to reduce speed and take it easy. Time was of no particular importance and he desired to establish the cows on their new pastures in good physical shape. Losses would also be lessened if the animals were permitted to feed well and were not exhausted by an effort beyond their endurance.

The morning of the third day out they were on unfamiliar range. Even Brady's knowledge of the country ahead was vague.

"Reckon it's up to me to scout out bedding-down sites," Hatfield observed.

"Reckon so," Brady admitted. "Any time you say, I'll take over on that chore."

"Oh, I don't mind," Hatfield replied. "I like to ride alone and, besides, old Goldy needs to stretch his legs."

He patted the great sorrel's arching neck as he spoke and was rewarded by a playful nip at his leg by milk-white teeth.

"He's sure a fine looking horse — can't

say as I ever saw a finer," Brady admired.

Later in the day, as Hatfield rode far in advance of the great herd, his chief concern was water which was not easy to come by in this dry land, yet was absolutely essential to the herd's welfare. More than a day's forced march without water would mean serious losses of weight.

So Hatfield eyed with interest every gulch and canyon opening onto the trail route. Some he investigated in the hope of finding a hidden spring. But as the afternoon wore on he began to have a disquieting premonition of a dry camp for the night.

He passed a wide, brushgrown canyon, the sloping sides of which were also with growth. For a moment he hesitated, but decided against riding up it. No stream flowed from its mouth and the growth had a parched look that was not promising. He rode on, his keen eyes scanning the terrain in all directions.

Something less than a quarter of a mile farther on the trail curved around a bulge, then straightened for a considerable distance to approach a second bend. And suddenly from around that bend bulged half a dozen horsemen. A bullet yelled through the air scant inches from his head.

Hatfield did not hesitate. Odds of six-to-one were a little heavy on the wrong side. He whirled Goldy and went streaking back the way he had come, bending low in the saddle as lead screeched all around him. He swore angrily as a slug burned his arm.

He was not particularly concerned, however. He was confident of his horse's great speed and endurance and had little doubt that he could soon put a safe distance between him and the unknown gun slingers. Already the range was too great for anything like accurate shooting from a running horse's back and barring a lucky hit, the pursuers had little to bank on.

Hatfield suffered no illusion as to the reason for the apparently wanton attack.

"That infernal image again," he told Goldy. "Are those hellions going to keep tabs on me clean across Texas? I don't like this, not one bit. They know darn well they can't outrun you. They've got something up their sleeve. Feller, I'm scared we're on some sort of a spot. Keep your eyes skun and help me look six ways at once."

Hatfield reached the bend in the trail with the pursuers steadily falling behind. Goldy was doing splendidly and appeared to enjoy the excitement of the chase. He tossed his head, snorted happily and literally poured his long body over the ground. His glorious black mane tossed and rippled in the wind of his passing. The sunlight struck glints of smouldering fire from his coat. His irons drummed the grass grown surface of the trail. They rounded the bend.

"I thought so!" Hatfield swore. Sweeping up from the southwest was a second band of horsemen — Hatfield counted seven in all. His appearance was the signal for more puffs of whitish smoke and the lethal whine of passing lead.

Hatfield's mind worked at hair-trigger speed. He could not turn, nor could he slant sideways into the south.

There was only one course left to him. On his left was a long, steep slope flinging upward to a rounded skyline. This slope was slashed by the canyon he passed on his outward ride. Without hesitation he swerved Goldy into the canyon and rode at top speed.

"Now if this hole just isn't a box, I've got a chance," he muttered, peering ahead as he tore through the brush that clothed the floor.

But he had a disquieting feeling that the canyon was boxed. It looked that way as it began to bend gently to the east. Behind him sounded shouts and a crashing of the growth. He settled himself in his saddle and urged Goldy to greater speed. If the canyon boxed, it was imperative for him to get a head start. Then perhaps he might find shelter or even try to ride up the steep slope.

After a sweeping curve, the canyon straightened out again. Hatfield swore under his breath. It was a box. Less than a half a mile ahead was a frowning, perpendicular wall.

The rough going didn't help Goldy any. Here his weight was a handicap. The pursuers, more lightly mounted, were gaining. Hatfield scanned the terrain ahead with anxious eyes. The growth was beginning to thin somewhat. Then he saw that it practically ended a hundred and fifty yards from the beetling box wall.

But about a score of yards from the wall was a glittering of huge boulders. He flashed toward them. They lay scattered clear across the width of the comparatively narrow gorge. Another moment and he was amid the weathered talus that had doubtless at some remote time fallen from the cliffs in the course of a natural convulsion or levin blast and rolled to their present position. He swerved Goldy behind one and dismounted, sliding his rifle stock against his cheek. His pale eyes glanced along the sights.

Smoke spurted from the muzzle. The clang of the report flung back and forth among the rocks. A man threw up his hands and plunged to the ground as if his horse had swallowed its head. Hatfield shifted the rifle muzzle the merest trifle and pulled trigger again. A second man went down. The others, with howls and curses, sent their mounts swerving into the thicker brush, hurling themselves from their saddles as they did so. The gorge rocked and trembled to the roar of gunfire. Bullets smacked against the boulders or ricocheted and whined off into space. Hatfield grimly raked the brush from side to side with a crackling volley. Crouching low, he stuffed fresh cartridges into the magazine.

A curious stillness had fallen, the more intense for the uproar that preceded it. The pursuers were lying low and holding their fire, realizing the futility of wasting lead against the granite barrier that sheltered the quarry. Hatfield also held his fire and lay tense and ready, every nerve strung to vibrating alertness.

Swiftly he estimated his position and calculated his chances. He was safe from a frontal attack but his flanks were exposed and fatally vulnerable. The space between where he lay and the cliff face was empty of growth, while the encroaching slopes were thickly brushed. There was nothing to prevent the attackers from crawling up the slopes and working around until they had him for an easy target. It was only a matter of time. Intently he surveyed the brush clad walls.

On the slope to his right and some fifty or sixty yards down canyon a bird suddenly whirled into view, darting and swooping over the bristle of thicket. Hatfield could hear its shrill, disturbed cries.

"There they go," he muttered, "working up through the brush. They flushed that bird. This is getting too darned interesting for comfort."

A panicky wave swept over him, but he mastered it sternly and forced himself to think. Quickly he evolved a plan, a desperately daring plan with a slim chance of success. His hope rested on a single factor. He counted on the eagerness of all the outlaws, stimulated by the excitement of the chase, to be in on the kill.

"If they just left only one or two men down here to hold the front, it might work," he told himself. He removed his hat and balanced it on the muzzle of his rifle. Turning sideways a little, he thrust the hat beyond the edge of his sheltering boulder.

A rifle banged instantly. The bullet brushed the crown of the hat as he jerked it back. His keen eyes detected the tiny wisp of smoke rising from a patch of growth directly in front and a little to the left.

"Got *you* spotted," he apostrophized the hidden rifleman. "Now let's see if there are any more."

He wiggled the hat around the opposite edge of the boulder, striving to simulate a man peering out to survey the ground ahead.

Again the rifle cracked. Hatfield noted with intense satisfaction that the smoke wisp arose from the same patch of growth as had the first. He rose to his feet and glided to where his horse stood regarding him with questioning eyes. He thrust the rifle into the boot, loosened his sixes in their holsters and gripped the split reins.

"If I've got this thing figured right and there's only one of the devils watching down there, I've got a chance," he told himself. "If I'm wrong, I'm dead."

He flung himself into the saddle, shouted to his horse. Instantly the great sorrel shot forward. Hatfield swung far down to the right behind the horse's neck and drew his right-hand gun.

The unseen rifle cracked. A slug yelled

past, fanning Hatfield's face with the wind of its passing. The big Colt boomed a drumroll of fire, raking the patch of brush with lead. He heard a yelp of pain. He swung over the other way as the rifle banged a second time and jerked his other gun. He was right on top of the patch of growth when a man sprang into view, blood streaming down his face, rifle levelled. Hatfield fired the instant before the other pulled trigger. The rifleman pitched sideways to lie in a huddled heap. Hatfield roared to Goldy and the sorrel scudded down the canyon like a lightning flash going places in a hurry. From the slopes on either side sounded yells and curses and the banging of guns.

But the growth was tall and thick and the outlaws could see little to shoot at. Another moment and Goldy was swerving around the bend and still going like the wind. Hatfield straightened up, ejected the spent shells from his guns and replaced them with fresh cartridges, chuckling to himself. Behind, the clamor of the frustrated outlaws dimmed and lessened. He bulged from the canyon mouth a little later and rode east at top speed. Glancing back, he saw horsemen emerging from the canyon far behind. A wrathful fist was shaken at him, then the whole band turned their horses and rode west.

9

Hatfield did not draw rein until he met the advancing herd. Tersely he regaled Brady and Kells with an account of what had happened. Brady swore in wrath and shook his fist.

"Roma's Raiders!" he declared. "They're out to get you, son!"

"Maybe," Hatfield agreed, "but there may be more to it. This herd stands for a sizable sum of money."

"It does that, all right," Brady agreed. He stared at the trail boss. "You mean to say you think they might make a try for the herd. With twenty men guarding it?" he scoffed.

"Well," Hatfield replied grimly, "twenty men are no better than five if they happen to be gotten into a position where they can be mowed down without being able to fight back. Perhaps the reason that bunch tackled me was to get me out of the way. You'd keep rolling along till you met me coming back or came to where I'd selected a bedding-down spot. The chuck wagons would have forged on ahead, and doing for the drivers would have been comparatively simple. Then the rest of you would have ambled right into an ambush. Don't forget, it isn't much more than a day's drive from here to the Rio Grande over a practically deserted section. And there's always a market down there for stolen stock. A bunch like Roma's would have their connections lined up in advance."

Old Brady swore explosively, and glared ahead.

"What you say makes sense, all right," he was forced to admit, "but today they sort of tipped their hand."

"Maybe," Hatfield admitted, "but will they think they tipped it. I've a good notion we haven't seen the last of that bunch. And it's up to us to see them before they see us, or at least to be ready for just such an eventuality."

"Sometimes you talk like a college professor," grumbled Brady, "but I reckon I get what you mean. Well, we'll keep our eyes open. But I can't for the life of me see how they'd figure to take us with outriders on the job all the time and scattered along the herd. You can't ambush a bunch of gents strung along a mile apart."

"But there are times when we may not be bunched," Hatfield observed. "I sure wish I knew the country ahead. Well, all we can do is take care to miss no bets. Double night guards from now on, and I don't figure to get over much sleep myself till we finish this drive."

A dry camp was made that night, some miles beyond the canyon in which Hatfield took refuge. Hatfield chose a spot where it would be impossible for anybody to approach the sleeping herd without being spotted by the alert night hawks. The following morning at daybreak the herd moved on. The cows were thirsty and restless and prone to stray. The riders had trouble keeping them to the trail.

Shortly after noon, Hatfield, Brady, Kells and a young puncher named Brown rode ahead in an anxious quest for water. As mile after mile was covered, their anxiety increased. Nowhere was there any indication of a stream or spring.

The country had changed. Now the semblance of a trail wound through low hills whose parched slopes rolled upward to the hard blue of the skyline. As they advanced, the encroaching slopes drew closer and closer together. They rounded a bend and saw, a mile ahead, the dark mouth of a narrow canyon with sloping, brush covered sides. Into this the trail ran.

As they neared the canyon, Brady exclaimed with satisfaction. Flowing from its mouth was a narrow, swift stream that crossed the trail and turned south into another rift in the hills.

At the canyon mouth they dismounted to drink and water their horses. Standing on the creek bank and rolling a cigarette, Hatfield surveyed the gloomy canyon through which they would be forced to pass. It was narrow. On either side, brush grown slopes rolled gently upward. Its floor was covered by a tall and dense stand of chaparral. Even the surface of the track was dotted with stray bushes. Some hundred yards beyond the mouth, Hatfield could see that the gorge curved somewhat to the south. He shook his head. The furrow between his black brows deepened slightly.

His companions did not need to be told what was in his mind. Their faces darkened as they gazed at the forbidding prospect.

"We'll have to bunch going through here," Hatfield observed. "No room for point men or flankers. It'll be everybody behind the herd while we're in that crack. I don't like it."

"It's a perfect set-up, all right," Brady agreed gloomily. "But we've got to go through. No running a herd over those sags. Too steep and too much brush."

Hatfield nodded, absently gazing at the hurrying water at his feet. Suddenly he leaned forward, concentrating on something that came bobbing and dipping over the ripples. It was a small whitish cylinder with one end seared to a rusty brown. Even as Hatfield stared, it unrolled into a bit of thin paper from which spilled brownish particles that quickly sank. The paper whirled and grayed as the water seeped into its substances and a moment later was swirled from sight by the current.

"Did you see it?" Hatfield exclaimed.

"Got a glimpse of it before it sank," Kells replied. "Looked like a cigarette butt."

"That's exactly what it was," Hatfield replied. "And it was chucked into the creek no great distance above here. Otherwise it would have opened up and sank before it got this far down. There's somebody up that hole. May mean nothing — just a chuck-line riding cowhand or a stray prospector, maybe."

"But it might be somebody holed up and waitin'," Kells interpolated grimly.

"Exactly," Hatfield agreed. He stared at the canyon mouth with narrowed eyes.

"Shall we slip in there and see?" young Brown suggested.

Hatfield shook his head. "Too risky," he said. "If there is somebody in there, waiting, they'll be keeping a sharp watch down canyon. Be almost sure to spot us."

He turned and gazed up the long brush covered slope to the north.

"I've a notion we could ride up that sag without much trouble," he said slowly.

"Reckon we could," agreed Brady. "What's on your mind, Jim?"

"If we can get up there without being spotted and then slide along parallel to the canyon, I've a notion we could work down the slope till we could see what's on the floor," Hatfield said. "If there are some devils down there waiting for the herd to come along, chances are they will be in the open. They would be able to hear the herd coming long before it gets here. Those thirsty cows are making plenty of noise. Then they'd take cover and be all set when we came ambling along behind the herd."

"But won't they think it funny nobody came scouting ahead?" asked Brown, the young puncher.

Hatfield shook his head. "What would you

do if you were scouting a thirsty herd and came to this crack?" he asked.

"Why, I'd hightail back and tell the Boss to shove the cows along fast 'cause I'd found water," Brown replied.

"Right," Hatfield nodded. "And I'm playing a hunch that is just what they've figured out. They'd know the herd would be watered here and then shoved on — long time till dark — and bed down somewhere on the creek bank either in the canyon or beyond it. Come on, we'll play that hunch."

They mounted and sent the horses struggling up the slope until they were a good six hundred yards above the canyon floor. Then they rode parallel to the gorge, carefully taking advantage of all possible cover. They passed the bend in the canyon and rode on a little farther until they hit upon a cleared space walled about by dense thicket.

"We'll leave the horses here and slip down the slope on foot," Hatfield decided. "They'd be sure to hear the horses popping the brush if we stay mounted. I figure right here on the far side of the bend would be their prime spot for a holeup. Careful now, and don't make any noise."

They tethered the horses, hoping the animals would not take a notion to sing any songs, and diagonalled down the sag on foot, careful to break no branch, to dislodge no stone that might roll and announce their presence. It was slow and hot work through the dense growth, but as they approached the canyon floor the chaparral stand thinned somewhat.

Suddenly Hatfield, who was in the lead, pulled up with a low exclamation. He pointed through a rift in the growth. His companions crowded eagerly behind him.

Through the rift they had a clear view of the canyon floor. Their eyes gleamed as they saw, lounging about on the open space of the old track, close to which ran the stream, a dozen or more men. Horses stood over to one side. The men were smoking and talking, but the cowhands were too distant to catch the words. Faces were little more than whitish blurs. The growth in the canyon had thinned greatly but was still ample to provide cover for the rustlers.

For long minutes, Hatfield studied the idling group, his brows drawing together.

"It's them, all right," he whispered. "All set and waiting. Soon as they hear the herd coming, they'll take cover on either side of the trail. That way we would have been mowed down!"

Brady was cursing steadily under his breath. His face was black with anger.

"Shall we let the skunks have it?" he whispered.

Hatfield shook his head. "Too many of 'em," he said. "They'd either take cover and smoke us out or they'd cut and run and most of 'em would get away. No, I've got a better scheme. Brown, you slip back to the horses. Fork your bronk and hustle back to meet the herd. Tell the boys what is up. Tell them to cut out about fifty cows and send 'em along fast. Tell 'em to roll the critters up the canyon, fast. Then when they hear us open the ball from up here, tell them to come a-foggin'. That way we'll catch the devils between fires and should bag every one of 'em."

"Fine! Fine!" applauded old Brady. "Hustle, Brown. Have four men stay with the main herd and shove it along. They'll have their hands full but they'll have to make out somehow."

Brown stole back into the growth. The others made themselves as comfortable as possible and waited, deadly rifles ready for instant action. In their hearts was nothing of mercy, in their minds no thought of giving the outlaws warning and a fighting chance for their lives. Those were stern times and men who rode with death as a constant stirrup companion held life cheaply. When men thought nothing of killing under the impact of a careless word or a card filched from a poker deck, what hope was there for rustlers and robbers, the enemies of all honest men, caught in the very commission of their crimes? Grim and expectant they waited for the first sound of the approaching cattle.

After a long and tedious wait it came, thin with distance, the querulous bleat of a tired and disgusted steer. They tensed for action.

The outlaws heard it, too. Instantly they were alert. Unconscious of the threat of those black muzzles on the slope above, they took up places in the brush. They were effectually concealed from anybody riding the trail, but easily spotted by the watchers on the slope.

Louder and louder grew the sounds of the approaching herd, the bleating and bawling, then the low pound of hurrying hoofs.

"Wait till you see the cows coming around the bend," Hatfield cautioned. "Then the boys will be right on top of them before they get over what we'll hand them!"

In the gorge below, the outlaws seemed to sense that something was not just right. The approaching cattle were coming too fast. The watchers on the slope could see them turning their heads to call to one another.

One or two stood up, peering down canyon with out-thrust necks.

Around the bend bulged a forest of tossing horns and rolling eyes as the frantic cattle strove to escape the lashing of quirts and the snapping of slickers in their rear.

"Let 'em have it!" barked Hatfield. The crash of his rifle echoed his voice as he pulled trigger as fast as he could work the ejection lever. Men went down. Others howled their alarm, leaping from their places of concealment, terrified, bewildered, unable to ascertain from whence the storm blast of death was coming. And before they could recover from their demoralization, the charging cowboys were on top of them, six-guns roaring.

The canyon was a pandemonium, a shambles. Smoke fogged upward. The ground was dotted with bodies. The cattle surged and milled in wild confusion. The cowboys yelled and whooped and blazed away at running figures.

From the bedlam of sound and action burst five men, racing for the snorting, bucking horses tethered to the right of the trail. A bullet whirled the hat from the head of one, revealing a head of black hair, as he mounted a plunging horse, the others close behind him.

"After them!" roared Hatfield.

Heedless of brush, thorns and rolling boulders, Hatfield charged down the slope, both guns roaring. But long before he reached the canyon floor, the outlaws had vanished from sight.

He bounded across to where the riderless horses were still plunging and snorting. He flung himself onto the back of one and charged in pursuit of the escaping raiders. Instantly, he and his companions were engulfed in the whirling tangle of the maddened cattle. It took minutes to fight free.

"Hold it!" Hatfield shouted. "They've got a head start and doubtless they know the country, which we don't. No sense in taking needless chances. Look those bodies over and see if you can recognize any of them."

After an inspection, there was a general shaking of heads.

"Well, we thinned 'em out a little, anyhow," the Lone Wolf said. "But I'm ready to swear that big black-haired hellion was the same man I saw up on the desert."

"Roma, sure as hell," swore old Brady.

"Maybe," Hatfield conceded. "Guess we might as well clean up a bit and bed down right here. I've a notion we'll make the rest of this drive in peace."

They did. The cattle were delivered and

paid for. Three days later saw everybody back safe on the home range.

Hatfield found things running smoothly at the mine. The day after getting back to the valley, he and Kells rode to town on an important errand. After eating, they repaired to the railroad station to await the arrival of the westbound train.

"That darn train is late, nearly half an hour," Kells observed. "She's usually right on the button."

Other citizens appeared to be of the same opinion. A considerable crowd had gathered about the station, craning necks to gaze along the twin ribbons of steel stretching into the east until they appeared to merge as one before curving out of sight around a bulge.

Among those present were Sheriff Walsh and two of his deputies. The sheriff appeared ill at ease and was constantly looking at his watch between glances shot eastward. He waved to Kells and Hatfield but did not offer to join them.

"Sheriff Tom is waitin' to guard the mines' payday money to the bank," Kells observed. "They have a big payroll over to the west and almost always the dinero is sent in from Rio the day before. That's what Walsh is here for, all right. He wouldn't have Jasper and Gaunt with him like that if he was just hangin' around to watch the train come in."

Another ten minutes passed, with the parallel ribbons of steel stretching empty into the east.

"Here she comes!" Kells suddenly exclaimed. "Look at her smoke!"

Around the distant curve bulged a bouncing black dot with a dark plume rolling back behind it. It rapidly increased in size. A moment later came, thin with distance, a long, frantic sounding whistle note, followed by a series of short toots.

"Look at her come!" chuckled Kells. "She's makin' up time for fair."

"Why," exclaimed somebody, "that isn't the train. That's just an engine by itself."

Hatfield had already noted the fact. His black brows drew together, his eyes narrowed a trifle as he saw that the pilot was smashed to kindling wood, the boiler front cracked and battered.

On came the racing locomotive, whistle blaring, exhaust thundering. It roared up to the station and halted with a screeching of brakes. While the engine was still in motion, a blue-clad figure dropped from the cab.

"The payroll money!" howled the conductor. "They got it! They shot the messenger and blowed the safe and hightailed. The express car is off the iron. We cleared the stuff they'd piled on the track and cut the engine loose and highballed for town."

A wild hubbub followed. Sheriff Walsh, by strident bellowing, got something like order.

"Who did it?" he shouted. "Where'd it happen? Where'd they go?"

"It was Roma and his bunch, who else?" howled the conductor. "They blocked the track on that big curve over east of the hills. They headed north by west."

"Are you plumb loco?" bawled the sheriff. "There's no place to go that way. A goat can't climb them cliffs. And north of the hills, to the west, is that blankety-blank desert. Yuh sure they didn't go east or south?"

"Yuh think my eyes are goin' back on me?" shouted the conductor in injured tones. "I had a company examination last month. They went north, veerin' west around the hills. We watched 'em out of sight. They were sure siftin' sand. Ain't yuh goin' after 'em?"

The sheriff swore till the air crackled. "They got better than an hour's start already," he said. "What chance I got to pick up their trail and foller it before dark? Is the messenger dead?"

"Sure he's dead," snorted the conductor. "They drilled him dead center. Put a hole in the baggagemaster's arm, too. They blowed that safe clean through the roof and peppered the coaches with lead till everybody was layin' on the floor. There was a dozen of 'em."

"Masked?"

"Of course they wore masks. Roma's bunch always wears masks."

The sheriff swore again, in helpless fury. Citizens crowded around with advice that tended but to increase his rage.

Jim Hatfield strode through the crowd, towering over those around him. He took the sheriff by the arm and drew him aside.

"Walsh," he said, "are you game to play a long hunch?"

"I'm game to play anything," growled the sheriff. "What yuh talkin' about?"

"Just this," Hatfield replied. "Get a posse together and head up Sanders Canyon. I got a prime hunch the hellions will head back to town by way of the canyon. If they do, you got a good chance to loop the lot of them."

The sheriff stared incredulously. "Now you done gone loco," he declared with conviction.

"Listen," Hatfield urged. "I had a run-in

with a bunch the day I came to this section across the Tonto. They chased me into the canyon. I went down over a bench and a sag where they were scairt to follow me. As soon as I was out of range, they turned and went hightailing north along the canyon rim like they knew just where they were going. I figured they were heading for a place where they could ride into the canyon. I noticed plenty of hoof marks in that canyon, nearly all of them leading south. And I'd swear the bunch that jumped me was Roma's outfit. If they can get into the canyon by circling to the north, it would be plumb simple for them to slip into town by ones and twos after it gets dark."

Sheriff Walsh tugged his mustache viciously. He glared at Hatfield and got the full force of the Lone Wolf's steady eyes in return. He tugged again, rumbled in his throat.

"By gosh," he exclaimed, at length, "for all I know you may be Roma hisself, but just the same I can't help feelin' yuh might have somethin' there. Will you go along as a special?"

"Sure," Hatfield replied. "Be glad to. And so will Kells. With your two deputies and four or five more straight shooting gents, we'll be all set."

"Let's go!" yelped the sheriff. "We got nothin' to lose but a mite of ridin', and if you happen to be right — well, *you* sure won't lose nothin' by it I'm able ever to do for yuh. Come on!"

The sheriff quickly selected his men from the swarm of volunteers. In less than twenty minutes the posse thundered up the canyon followed by the remarks of the citizenry, most of them derisive.

"If this don't work out, I'll be laughed plumb out of town," the sheriff confided to Hatfield.

"I'm playing a hunch," the Ranger returned, "and I've a mighty good notion it's a straight one. I've noticed that a bunch apparently pulling mysterious things are usually found to be doing something plumb simple. If that bunch has got a get-away through the canyon, it explains how they've always been able to get in the clear after pulling something. Do you know anything about the upper end of the canyon?"

"Not over much," the sheriff admitted. "It's not the sort of a place folks go amblin' around in just for the fun of it, leadin' up into a desert like it does. But I have a notion it wouldn't be hard to get into up to the north. It must sort of peter out up there. No hills to box it. I've a notion some old timers hereabouts would know, but I'm from the southeast end of the county and not over familiar with this section."

One or two of the cowhands who made up the posse professed the belief that a descent into the canyon would be comparatively easy some twenty miles to the north.

"I was out on the desert up there a few years back," one said. "It's a helluva section, all right. I rec'lect riding down into a big gulch up there, hopin' to find water. I followed the draw for a ways, but it kept gettin' deeper and deeper, and dryer all the time, so I give it up. I've a notion that draw might lead into the canyon."

Hatfield nodded. "It would be perfect for an on-the-run bunch," he pointed out to the sheriff. "There's no trailing anything over the Tonto. Once out there, especially with a little wind blowing, and they'd be in the clear. Then with a private back door to town, they'd be sitting pretty."

"Sure hope yuh're right," grunted Walsh. "Well, we'd ought to find out one way or the other before long."

A little later, with the town well behind them, Hatfield ventured further advice.

"Slow down a bit," he told Walsh. "No sense in running our horses' legs off. If they're coming this way, they'll take it easy.

They won't want to make town before dark. What we're looking for is a proper place to hole up and wait for them. They can't turn aside anywhere, and I figure they won't begin splitting up till they're pretty close to Sanders."

The sheriff agreed without question. He did not appear to think it strange that Hatfield should be giving the orders and he obeying them. Nor did any of the possemen offer suggestions or objections.

They had covered nearly fifteen miles and the sun was already well down the western sky when Hatfield suddenly called a halt. The canyon had narrowed somewhat, the cliffs drawing together and overhanging. Here the brush thinned out leaving a comparatively open space some two hundred yards in width before the gorge widened and the growth began again.

"This is perfect," he told the others. "They'll come through this gut bunched and we'll have the drop on them. We'll be holed up and they'll be in the open. Run the horses well back into the brush and leave them. Then we'll take up positions here to cover the whole open space."

The posse took up positions as Hatfield directed. A tedious wait ensued. Slowly the hours passed. The canyon became shadowy with advanced evening. Sheriff Walsh grew acutely uneasy.

"I hate to think what folks will say when we come back with an empty sack," he muttered.

"You're not back yet," Hatfield told him. "Take it easy, now."

Another half hour passed, with the gloom increasing in the narrow gorge and the sheriff's gloom increasing in direct ratio.

"We won't be able to shoot in another ten minutes," Kells muttered.

Suddenly Hatfield held up his hand. The others heard it, too, a faint clicking sound.

"Get set!" the Ranger said in low tones. "Here they come. Walsh, you do the talking when I give the word, not before."

The clicking swiftly loudened to the beat of a number of horses' irons moving at a good pace, but unhurriedly. There was a crackling in the brush ahead. A body of men rode into view, a dozen or more. Riding carelessly at ease, they cantered forward across the open space.

"All right," Hatfield whispered to Walsh. "Tell it to 'em!"

Instantly the sheriff's stentorian bellow blared forth —

"In the name of the law! Halt! You are under arrest!"

Followed a storm of exclamations, a clashing of hoofs and a jangle of bit irons as the approaching horsemen jerked their mounts to a halt. Hands flashed to belts.

"Let 'em have it!" Hatfield thundered. Both his guns let go with a stunning roar.

Yells, shrieks and curses arose. The narrow gorge fairly exploded to the crash of gunfire.

The owlhoots were backing their horses and blazing away at the dimly seen possemen. Four of their saddles had been emptied by the first deadly volley. Almost instantly two more men were down. A voice rang out, clear, preemptory —

"Back! Hightail! It's a trap!"

The remaining outlaws whirled their horses. Hatfield leaped forward, heedless of the lead storming around him. He fired again and again till the hammers of his guns clicked empty shells. Beside him, Kells and the sheriff were shooting as fast as they could pull trigger.

In a moment it was over. Five riders, bending low in their hulls, went crashing into the brush to the north. Riderless horses were milling and dashing in every direction. Seven forms lay sprawled on the canyon floor.

"After 'em!" yelled the sheriff. But Hatfield instantly countermanded the order.

"They've got a head start," he told Walsh. "It'll take time to go for our horses, and it'll be black dark in ten minutes. They know the ground, and we don't. They'd either beat us to the way out or they'd hole up somewhere and mow us down as we came floundering along in the dark. Look the bodies over and catch those horses. Their saddle pouches look full. Anybody hurt bad?"

One posseman had a hole through the fleshy part of his upper arm. Another had suffered a bullet gashed cheek. A slug had burned a streak along the ribs of a third.

"Nothing serious," Hatfield observed thankfully as he proceeded to stanch the flow of blood from the punctured arm and bind it up.

"What did you find, Walsh?" he called in answer to an excited whoop from the sheriff.

"These pouches are plumb stuffed with dinero," the sheriff boomed back. "By gosh, I've a notion we got darn nigh the whole lot of the payroll money back."

"That's good," Hatfield replied. "What about those hellions on the ground?"

"All done for, proper," Kells reported. "I'm sure I've seen a couple of 'em in town hangin' around the saloons."

"Me, too," added a posseman. "I remember three of 'em. One I played poker with once in the Ace-Full. He said he rode for an outfit over in the Bend. Didn't look like he'd handled a rope or an iron for quite a spell, I rec'lect."

However, nobody could recall anything but vague recollections of having seen one or the other of the dead men in town. Hatfield could learn nothing relative to their associations, if any.

"One thing is about sure, Roma ain't one of 'em," growled the sheriff. "None of 'em got the look of bein' able to run an outfit like his. Border scum, all of 'em."

"I've a large notion it was Roma we heard yelling to the others to hightail," observed Hatfield.

"Chances are yuh're right," agreed the sheriff. "His sort always does the quick thinkin'."

"If they'd only showed ten minutes earlier," lamented Kells. "Then we would have got a good look at all of 'em. As it was, their faces were just white blurs in the dark."

The pockets of the dead men turned out nothing of significance, but the sheriff exulted over the contents of the saddle pouches.

"And we sure put a crimp in Roma's tail,"

he crowed. "Busted his gang all to blazes. Reckon we won't hear much of that sidewinder for a spell."

"But the head of the snake got away," Hatfield marked to Kells. "And that sort of a head grows another body in a hurry."

After roping the bodies to the backs of the horses, Sheriff Walsh waddled over and solemnly shook hands with Jim Hatfield.

"Feller," he said, "if yuh have another hunch, bring it around and I'll foller it till hell freezes over and pigs walk across on the ice. All right, boys, we might as well head back to town. I'm gettin' hungry."

Excitement was great in Sanders when the posse arrived with the bodies and more than two thirds of the money looted from the express car. Several citizens, including bartenders and other tradesmen, were convinced that they had seen one or another of the slain owlhoots before, but could add nothing more of value.

"The darn town has been full of mavericks comin' and goin' ever since the gold strike," growled Sheriff Walsh. "Was bad enough even before that. This is a handy stopover point for that sort. The nerve of 'em, to hole up here right under my nose!"

They learned that a wreck train had gotten the derailed express car back on the track so that the delayed Flyer could continue on its belated way.

"Hope Mary got her Chinese cook to the ranch before Stuffy Jones killed somebody with his messes," chuckled Kells. "Sauerkraut boiled in coffee!"

Sheriff Walsh and the possemen industriously spread around the story of the successful maneuver and Hatfield was the recipient of admiring glances as he and Kells ate a late supper together.

"You're gettin' plenty of attention, feller," the mine owner chuckled.

"Yes, and some of it may be the sort I won't relish," the Ranger returned grimly.

"Uh-huh," Kells agreed. "I've a notion quite a few gents in this pueblo won't feel over friendly toward yuh, or to the rest of us, for that matter. But I can't help feelin' pretty good about it all. Quite a few gents who have been lookin' the other way when I passed by of late have made it a point to come up and speak to me. Looks like I'm gettin' deeper and deeper in your debt all the time."

10

Hatfield and Kells spent the night in town, and experienced no untoward incident. The next morning, a coroner's jury speedily justified the slaying of the seven owlhoots and recommended that the sheriff run down the rest of the varmints as speedily as possible.

"Payday will be a day late this month," Kells observed as they rode back to the Tumbling K. "And if it hadn't been for you, it would have been more than a day late. The bank wouldn't have been able to handle the payroll for all the mines without the dinero we recovered."

Hatfield nodded, his eyes on the country around. Abruptly he asked a question.

"The other day, while we were riding out to your place," he remarked, "you mentioned that Bern Cowdry's father got killed in Arizona. How did it happen?"

Kells hesitated before replying.

"I ain't much on passin' around talk I ain't sure about," he said at length. "The story goes that Chet Cowdry got hisself plugged during a stage hold-up. I ain't sure it's true, but that's how the talk goes. Chet was always the black sheep of a good family, it 'pears. Had trouble with his brother, got mixed up in crooked gamblin' and left this section, years back. Walt Cowdry never talked much about him. He was a salty hombre, all right, and I reckon young Bern takes after him. But nobody has ever knowed Bern to do anything off color. He's worked hard and behaved himself proper since he showed here. Reckon it ain't fair to hold what his dad may have done against him. That's why I didn't mention how Chet Cowdry got took off when I was talkin' to you the other day. Fact is, about the only thing Bern ever does out of the way is gamble. He likes cards, plays considerable in town, and never seems to have much luck. Him and old Walt had some rows over that, I understand. Walt was dead set against gamblin' in any form. He said gamblin' was what ruined his brother. He said Chet was all right till he took to foolin' with cards and finally ended up in a shootin' and had to cut and run. Reckon he was scairt Bern might get into a ruckus of that sort. Bern's a hot-tempered jigger."

Hatfield nodded again. "I see," he said. "No, it isn't right to blame anybody for what someone else does, even if he does happen to be a member of the same family. Most every family can drop a loop on a maverick belonging to them, if they look back far enough."

"That's so," Kells agreed soberly. "Well, here we are, and everything looks to be under control. Reckon they ain't had no trouble since we been gone."

Kells removed the sack of payroll money from his saddle pouch and stowed it away in his small office safe. Then they inspected mine and mill and found everything going smoothly.

"And now, feller, I'm goin' to ask a real favor of yuh," Kells said when they returned to the office. "Reckon yuh're good at figures, seein' as yuh're so good at everything else. I ain't, and makin' up that darn payroll is a plumb awful chore for me. Think you could handle it this afternoon?"

"Reckon I can bear up under the strain," Hatfield smiled reply.

"Plumb much obliged," Kells said gratefully. "I'll get yuh the time sheets. The money's in the safe and here is the combination on this slip of paper. Seein' as you're takin' over, I'll ride around a mite this afternoon and see how things are goin' on the spread."

After eating, Hatfield settled himself to the task of office work. Kells would have been astonished had he seen how easily and quickly the Lone Wolf did away with the "plumb awful chore." An hour after sitting down at the desk, Hatfield put the filled and identified envelopes in the safe, closed it and rolled himself a cigarette. As he was fumbling out the makin's, his hand struck against the small golden image with the opal eyes. He drew it forth and glanced at it.

"Reckon I might as well stow this thing in the safe, too," he decided. "Better than packin' it around with me. I'll just poke it back in one of the compartments and nobody will notice it there."

By the bright sunlight streaming through the window, he examined the thing again. The line of jointure where the peg of stone fitted into the base was very fine and showed every indication of crafty workmanship. He rasped the slightly rough surface of the stone with his finger nail.

"Been busted loose from something, all right," he mused. He hefted the image in his palm. Suddenly he was struck by an idea.

He located a rule in the desk and carefully measured the image, noting its dimensions on a sheet of paper. Then he set it aside and did some figuring. Next he meticulously adjusted the balances of the assay scales on a nearby table. He placed the image in the pan and weighed it on the scales so sensitive that, Hatfield knew, if he weighed a two-inch scrap of paper on them and then wrote his name on the paper with a coarse pencil and weighed it again, the scales would take notice of the addition. He jotted down the result and compared it with what his measuring and figuring had attained. Then he uttered an exclamation of satisfaction.

"Thought the darn thing was light for its size," he muttered. "It's hollow. Here goes for another hunch."

Eyes glowing with interest, he went to work on the base of the image with the point of his knife.

Dislodging the stone plug was considerable of a chore, but he finally accomplished it. A small round hole showed where the plug had fitted snugly into the soft metal.

Hatfield turned the image upright and shook it. A silky rustling rewarded his efforts. He tapped the base against the table top, shook it again.

From the opening dropped a tiny roll of

parchment-like paper tied with a thread of fibre. He undid the knot and carefully spread the sheet.

Written on the surface in faded ink were faint but decipherable Spanish words. He read them without difficulty.

In *Valle de la Luna* (he read) is stored — (followed several illegible words) against the day when the people will rise and drive the invader from the land of Anahuac and restore the ancient Gods to their wonted places. May the curse of Metzli, the curse of Huitzelcoatl, the curse of Quetzalcoatl be upon him who betrays the sacred trust, in this world, in the world beyond the stars, in the world beyond the world beyond the stars.

"For the love of Pete!" Hatfield exclaimed. He turned the paper over. On the opposite side were seemingly meaningless lines.

But as he gazed on the dim strokes, they slowly took form to become an undoubted map of the wide walled canyon known as Moon Valley. At the upper end of the canyon was a small circle marked *Caverna* — Cave.

Hatfield stared at the drawing, a smile on his lips.

"So this is what they were after," he

chuckled. "Buried treasure! A perfect set-up: the ancient writing, the hidden map, everything. Uh-huh, buried Aztec gold. Huitzelcoatl was the Aztec god of war. Quetzalcoatl was the great god of the air. Metzli was the god of the underworld. Chances are this thing is a translation, perhaps from the Aztec writing of the knotted cords. Plumb perfect. And the chances are a hundred to one it doesn't mean a thing. The Southwest is full of such legends and campfire yarns and tall stories, handed down from father to son for generations. But men will rob and kill for a thing like this."

He fingered the crackling paper, his eyes serious again.

"But it is liable to prove useful," he mused. "I figure they'll make another try for it, and that may give me a chance to drop my loop. The thing is beginning to tie up. Old Miguel, the Cowdry cook, for that's who that Mexican was, no doubt about it — old Miguel must have gotten hold of the image somehow, stole it, the chances are. Knew what was inside of it. Somehow or other, Roma and his bunch got onto it and set out to get it. Miguel hightailed and they lot out to hunt for him. But between that darn snake and me, they didn't get it. Begin to see now why somebody is so anxious to ease Kells out of Moon Valley so they can get hold of the valley and do their hunting uninterrupted. Everything in the valley belongs to Kells, of course. Evidently they knew the secret was inside the image."

He paused from his reflections to roll a cigarette.

"And," he added grimly, "I'm getting a mighty good notion who Roma is. Nobody but Bern Cowdry. Bern Cowdry, the son of an owlhoot, the man who brought Miguel to the Cross C spread. Well, he looks the part, all right. The big jigger I figured to be Roma wasn't at all. I could swear that wasn't Cowdry. Blazes, that could have been Purdy! They said he was always riding off somewhere. Let's see, now. Yes that was a Sunday, and he wouldn't be working on a Sunday.

"And I'm beginning to see what Bern Cowdry was up to when he braced Kells out there on the trail. He knew he could beat Kells to the draw. He figured to do for Kells, and do for me at the same time. He knew I had the image on me. It would have been perfect. Talk about a snake-blooded hellion!"

For some time he sat smoking. Finally he pinched out his cigarette, restored the map to the image and replaced the stone plug. He wrapped the figurine in a handkerchief and stowed it away in the safe behind some papers.

Absorbed in the task and his thoughts, he did not see the face peering in through the open window, a face that faded from sight before he turned around.

"Tomorrow is payday and there won't be any work," he mused. "Think I'll take myself a little ride just to prove this buried treasure business is all the plumb nonsense I figure it is."

Kells returned to the ranchhouse just after sundown.

"Everything going fine," he told Hatfield. "The boys are handling their chores all right. I'll be set to make a good beef shipment soon which will help."

The following morning the mine and mill workers rolled off to town in ore wagons. The cowboys, whooping and skylarking, rode with them.

"Be sore heads tomorrow, but they'll be happy," Kells chuckled as he and Hatfield watched them go. "Sort of nice to be on your own and have no responsibilities. Well, a feller has to pay for everything he gets in this world one way or another. I think I'll ride in myself, late this afternoon. Want to come along? The night watchman will be here to keep an eye on things."

"If you don't mind," Hatfield replied, "I'd like to take a ride up the valley today. I'd like to look your range over. Not used to being cooped up inside. After all, I was brought up on a spread and am sort of used to riding."

"You'll enjoy it," Kells instantly enthused. "She's a plumb fine little spread, feller, and it'd do any cowman good to look her over. Okay, I'll see you when I get back tonight if yuh haven't gone to bed. Otherwise, tomorrow mornin'."

About mid-morning, Hatfield got the rig on Goldy and rode off up the valley at a leisurely pace. Very quickly he decided that Kells had not exaggerated in speaking of his holdings. It was really beautiful rangeland. A fairly broad and deep creek flowed down the west side of the valley, gradually edging toward the center, as Hatfield approached its source at the head of the canyon. The grass was tall and there were plenty of groves and thickets. Narrow draws and arroyos pierced the side walls to provide ample shelter against heat and storms. The cows were sleek and well fleshed. Hatfield could readily understand Kells' desire to hold the valley above all else.

"Feller was born and brought up a cowhand," he mused. "Got grass rope and horse in his blood. Never be satisfied away from them. Well, the way his mine is producing, he shouldn't have any trouble meeting all his obligations and getting plumb free title to his holdings here.

"And," he added, with a chuckle, "if I can just get this confounded mess in this section straightened out, I've a notion that little blue-eyed gal with the yellow hair will be helping him run it before long."

As he worked north, the canyon gradually narrowed. The perpendicular side walls were replaced by long, fairly steep brush grown and boulder strewn slopes slashed by gloomy side canyons.

"A regular hole-in-the-wall country up here," he mused. "The sort of a place all kinds of yarns build up about."

Finally he reached the canyon's head, a brush grown gorge studded with chimney rocks and only a few hundred yards wide. The end wall of the box was a beetling, perpendicular cliff nearly a hundred feet in height.

Hatfield rode slowly along the cliff face to the west wall, turned and rode back to the east wall, an amused smile on his lips. Nowhere was there a cave, nor any indications that one had ever existed. The stream that flowed down the valley came plunging over the end wall in a feathery plume to foam and thunder in the catch basin at the cliff's base.

"The same old story," Hatfield chuckled. "Just something built up by a joker or somebody with a plumb valid imagination. Well, it's what I expected. If all the gold indicated on these old maps and told about and written about really existed and was turned up, we'd be using the darn stuff to make boot scrapers."

He hooked one long leg comfortably over the saddle horn, rolled and lighted a cigarette. For some minutes he sat smoking, listening to the thunder of the falling water and admiring its graceful curve over the tall cliff crest. Finally he pinched out the butt, cast it aside and rode back down the gorge chuckling to himself. A quarter of a mile or so down canyon, he halted Goldy, turned and gazed at the pluming fall.

Suddenly his eyes grew serious and he stopped chuckling. He stared at the fall, turned and studied the swiftly flowing creek. He turned back to the fall and gave it concentrated attention for some moments. Again he stared at the fairly broad and deep stream hurrying down the canyon.

"Blazes!" he muttered. "If my eyes aren't going back on me, and I don't figure they are, there's just about three times as much water in the crik as is coming over the cliff. Now what's the answer to that?"

The answer was fairly obvious to the Lone Wolf. If the plainly apparent volume of water in the stream did not come over the cliff, it must come through or from under it. Which incontrovertible fact opened up interesting possibilities. He turned Goldy and rode back to the end of the gorge, dismounted and approached the cliff face at the edge of the fall.

For some moments he studied the water foaming into the catch basin. He eyed the tremulous film of spray beating against the rock wall, then turned and led Goldy down to where the grass grew luxuriantly amid the stones. He removed the bit, let the split reins trail.

"Go ahead and fill yourself up," he told the sorrel. "I'll be seeing you in a little while, I hope."

He returned to the cliff face, drew a deep breath and stepped into the curtain of spray showering the rock. Two cautious steps and he was beyond the veil of water, standing on a narrow ledge and gazing straight at the downward-rushing green and gold main body of the fall.

As he knew was usual with a cataract, there was an air filled hollow between the falling water and the cliff.

But this time there was more. A dark opening yawned in the cliff face, from which rushed a torrent of water much greater in volume than the fall.

"And that's where most of the water in the crik comes from," he muttered. "This is getting interesting."

The subterranean stream did not fill the cave mouth. On either side was a rocky floor some yards in width.

Hatfield stepped into the opening and eased forward a little ways. As he progressed, the wonderful green-gold light that filled the mouth of the cave quickly dimmed. Ahead was only black darkness.

"Wish I had something that would do for a torch," he told himself, "but anything I was packing would have gotten drenched, anyhow," he added, shaking some of the water from his clothes and hat.

He drew a tightly corked bottle from his pocket, wiped it off and shook out a couple of matches. On his boot sole, close to the heel, was a dry patch of leather. He struck the match on it. The tiny flame, flaring up instantly and burning with a steady glow, revealed a solid rock wall at his elbow, smooth and dry. The light penetrated but a few feet into the cave, however. Beyond was black darkness.

Hatfield hesitated a moment, then stepped forward again, feeling his way cautiously against possible pitfalls. He knew he could not become lost so long as he kept close to the purling water's edge, but before he had covered two hundred yards distance the stream turned almost at right angles. He cautiously followed its course and butted up against the far wall. He struck another match and saw that the water gushed from under the side wall.

But this was not the end of the cave. The black bore stretched on ahead.

"Well, if I keep against the wall, I still can't get myself lost," he declared and moved ahead again.

He covered another hundred yards, slowly and carefully. The rock floor was perfectly smooth, with no apparent holes or loose stones. Instinctively he increased his pace a little under a feeling of false security.

The passage developed a gentle downward slope but remained smooth and unobstructed. Hatfield stepped out confidently. Then, with a gasp, he hurled himself backward and sideways as his outstretching foot encountered nothing but empty space. His other foot dashed against a loose fragment of stone and he pitched forward into the dark. A faint, sullen splash drifted upward from the abysmal depths of a gulf that split the cavern floor.

11

Weak and shaking, cold sweat dampening his face and his palms, Jim Hatfield lay where he had fallen across rough stone steps that plunged dizzily downward into the darkness, his legs hanging over the chasm, his back against the cave wall. For moments he did not dare move. Then slowly and carefully he inched his legs and feet back over the edge and got shakily to his feet. He drug out his matches and struck one.

Hugging the cavern wall, the steps stretched downward before him, a rough stair hewn with incalculable labor from the living rock. The gulf that lapped the outer edge was of unknown width.

"And from the sound sent back by that rock I kicked over the edge, it goes down to the front door of hell," he muttered. "Say, this is getting just a mite too interesting."

He struck another match and peered downward. For a moment he hesitated.

Reason said to go back the way he had come, but curiosity urged him to find out where the mysterious stair led.

Curiosity finally won out. With the greatest caution he began descending the stair, hugging the rock wall, testing each step before trusting his weight upon it.

The descent was a nightmare in the black dark. All desire to hurry left him and he crept downward at a snail's pace. At first he counted the steps, but soon lost track of their number. He developed a queer feeling that he was walking down an unfolding ribbon of eternity, without beginning and without end.

Abruptly he jerked his advancing foot back and hugged the wall. His boot had splashed in water.

He struck another match and peered ahead. Before him stretched a smooth, black expanse. No ripple disturbed its deathly still surface. It looked like the combined oozings from all the graves in the world. He hesitated again as the match flickered out and the black dark clamped down upon him with an intensity that could almost be felt.

"But whoever built this darn staircase didn't do it to reach a diving pool," he reasoned. "Of course the water may have settled here long after the stair was built.

May have no bottom, but reckon I'll take a chance. Doesn't appear to be any current and I should be able to swim back if it gets too deep."

He stepped into the pool and was surprised to find it was not unpleasantly cold. He could feel the steps still under his feet, but before the water rose much beyond mid-thigh they ended. His feet rested on a smooth, level surface. He took a cautious step forward, another. The water rose no higher.

The pool proved to be little more than twenty yards in width. It began to shallow and a moment later Hatfield found himself on dry ground. He peered ahead, but the darkness was still stygian. The flame of a match showed a narrow passage.

Again he began his cautious advance. Five minutes of slow groping passed and suddenly the darkness ahead began to gray. Swiftly the light grew stronger. The passage curved. He rounded the bulge and stood staring in astonishment.

The gloomy gallery had widened into a wide, almost circular amphitheatre of a cup. On all sides was a curving wall of dark stone. Only a few paces to the left was a chasm that seemed to drop down and down, depth upon vertiginous depth, to the earth's heart. Sunlight poured down from far, far above where the dark lip of the cup was rimmed with the deep blue of the Texas sky.

"An old crater," Hatfield exclaimed. "A minor blow-hole when this section was a scene of volcanic activity. Sort of like the Ashes Mountains country up around the Guadalupes. He turned and glanced around and uttered a low whistle as his eyes fell upon what crouched against the wall of black rock, protected by a crude overhang of the lava cliff above.

Winged and scaled, birdlike and serpentine, a great stone figure stared back at him with eyes of reddish quartz. Surmounting its feathered head-dress, fantastically carved from gray stone, was a gleaming crescent. Before it was the stone slab of an altar, the ominous blood channels scoring its surface.

"Metzli!" Hatfield exclaimed. "Metzli, the moon god. The Valley of the Moon. This was an old Aztec temple. Lots of them found over in the San Juan River Valley in New Mexico and quite a few in the Texas Big Bend country."

He stepped closer. Something apparently perched on the outer corner of the altar caught his eye. He stooped to examine it and uttered another exclamation.

The tiny gold figure was an exact replica

of the jewel-eyed image stored in the Tumbling K mill safe. He reached out and gave it a tug. With a sharp snapping sound it came free in his hand. There showed the clean, fresh cleavage of a broken stone peg driven into the base of the image. A fragment of the peg remained imbedded in the stone slab of the altar.

Hatfield examined the opposite corner of the altar. There, too, was the upright splinter of a broken stone peg, its surface dull and weathered.

"The one old Miguel gave me came from here," the Ranger exulted. "Was broken away a long, long time ago. Doubtless the story of the hidden map went with it. Somehow or other Miguel got hold of it and heard the legend connected with it. If this doesn't beat all!"

He pocketed the image and walked around the great stone statue. He paused, staring, and suddenly laughed aloud.

He was gazing on the hidden "treasure" of Moon Valley!

A deep niche had been hollowed in the lava rock, extending far around the wide curve of the cup. Stacked in the niche were row on row of spears tipped with copper, huge clubs set with spikes of obsidian, heavy copper swords, long bow staves, the strings long since rotted away, coats of lacquered mail, painted helms of hardwood, fashioned like the heads of pumas, wolves, snakes, and other implements of war.

"Stored against the day of the land of Anahuac's need!" Hatfield paraphrased the words written on the back of the ancient map. "Of course, what else? Gold meant nothing to the Aztecs. They used it only for ornaments and decoration. For them it held no real value. They were tillers of the soil and fighting men. Here in this secret place they stacked up arms against the day of war when they hoped to drive out the Spanish invaders. Some nice museum pieces here, but no buried gold. Say, it's a pity that bunch of sidewinders didn't manage to hit on this place. It would have been something to hear them cuss. Well, I've had a nice trip, with a laugh at the end of it. Reckon I'd better climb back up that snake hole and head for home and try and figure a way to drop a loop on those hellions. Nothing more to see here and no way out but up those rocks."

With a last glance at the grim stone god watching over his hidden "treasure" that would never be put to use, Hatfield re-entered the dark passage.

First, however, he plucked one of the old

bow staves from its place in the niche. The wood was tinder dry and when he touched a match to its tip, it burned with a steady flame.

With the aid of the improvised torch, crossing the pool and climbing the stair was easy. Just as the sun was sinking in scarlet and gold behind the west wall of the canyon, he stepped through the filmy edge of the waterfall to see his sorrel standing nearby and patiently awaiting him.

Still chuckling, Hatfield rode down the valley through the rose flecked blue of the approaching dusk. But his jovial mood soon left him. The treasure hunt, so called, had ended in a ludicrous anticlimax, but the grim business of dropping a loop on Roma and his bunch was still very real.

"That scaly varmint will bust loose some-place else in a hurry if he isn't hogtied," the Lone Wolf told his horse. "He's as fangin' as any rattler that ever coiled under a bush, and losing the payroll money won't set well with him. He'll be out to even up for that in a hurry. And I haven't got the least notion how to stop him. The suspicions I have aren't the sort of thing you can present in court and hope to get anywhere. A good lawyer would make me look as short of brains as a terrapin is of feathers. Well, maybe we'll get a break."

Even then the break was in the making, in a totally unexpected fashion.

Hatfield took his time down the valley, appreciating to the full the loveliness of the walled rangeland as the Master Painter limned the sky in crimson and mauve and molten bronze. The rim of the cliffs was ringed about with saffron light that crowned their robes of dusky purple as with an imperial diadem. Birds sang sleepily in the growth. Each twig tip was a gem of dying radiance, and as a strengthening wind rippled the grasses the wide expanse was a sea of drowsy emerald washed in gold.

"Looks like a change in weather," the Ranger told his horse. "Those clouds in the west are piling up fast. Well, reckon we could stand a mite of rain. Been sort of dry of late."

Finally the Tumbling K buildings came into view. Ranchhouse and bunkhouse were dark, but a glow of light showed in the office window of the mill, doubtless lit by the watchman Hatfield had posted since the night of the fire.

Hatfield turned Goldy's head toward the barn, but before he reached it, he heard a hoarse cry from the direction of the dark mill. He turned the sorrel quickly and rode toward the light that streamed through the office window.

A figure appeared in the door, clutching the jamb for support. It was the night watchman. His eyes were wild, his face caked with dried blood that had flowed from a jagged furrow splitting his scalp just above the right temple.

Hatfield pulled up and unforked in a ripple of movement. He went up the steps three at a time.

"What's the matter?" he asked.

"The hyderphobia skunk shot me," panted the watchman. "I come to in time to throw lead at him, but he dived through the window and got away. I heard his horse's irons clickin' as he hightailed."

Hatfield took the man by the arm, led him to the office and seated him in a chair. With deft fingers he examined the wound.

"No bones busted," was his diagnosis. "I'll tie it up and it will be okay. Now tell me what happened."

"I was just comin' into the mill, makin' my rounds," said the watchman. "I was in the passage outside the office. I just got a glimpse of him and there was a blaze of light and the roof fell in on me. He'd cut down on me and creased me. Must have figured he'd done me in. Reckon it was the dynamite goin' off that jolted the senses back in my head."

"The dynamite?"

The watchman gestured to a shadowy corner of the room. Hatfield glanced quickly in the direction indicated.

The door of the office safe, ripped from its hinges, lay against the wall. Papers were scattered over the floor.

"The jigger must have been after the payroll money," said the watchman. "Reckon he got his days mixed up and didn't know the boys were handed their envelopes this mornin'. Wasn't anything much in the box, was there?"

"Very little," Hatfield replied. He crossed to the rifled safe. Some coins and a few bills were scattered among the papers on the floor. He thrust his hand inside a certain compartment and felt about.

The tiny golden image of Metzli, the moon god, was gone.

12

Hatfield stood for a moment, thinking deeply.

"So there was still a third hellion working here in cahoots with Roma and his bunch," he muttered. "Must have seen me put the statue in there. Wonder how much he did see? A lot depends on that. If he saw me take the map out of the image, things may work out fine. I'm going to play a hunch in that direction, anyhow."

With a word to the injured watchman, he left the office. From his saddle pouch he procured a roll of bandage and a pot of antiseptic ointment. He got water and cleansed the watchman's wound, dressed it and bandaged it expertly.

"That had ought to hold you till you get to town and let the doctor look it over," he said. "Come on up to the house, now, and I'll rustle us a mite of chuck and some steamin' coffee. Reckon you can stand both, and I'm sort of empty myself.

"You did a good chore, feller, by coming to and throwing lead at that horned toad," he added. "Given time, he might have set fire to the mill or something. Let's go."

Hatfield first cared for his horse, then quickly made coffee and rustled a meal. They ate heartily to the accompaniment of thunder muttering and rumbling in the west. Hatfield rolled cigarettes for both of them and they smoked in comfortable silence. The Ranger pinched out his butt and stood up.

"I'm heading for town," he told the watchman. "You stay here in the house and rest that head. There'll be nothing more to worry about tonight. Keep your ears open, though. When you hear horses two or three hours from now, the chances are it will be me with the boss and some other jiggers. I'll let out a whoop as soon as we clear the brush. That will let you know it's us. If anybody else comes snooping around, there's a Winchester over there in the corner and a box of cartridges on the mantelpiece. Load her up and use her if things don't look right. I'll be seeing you."

Hatfield rode to Sanders at a fast pace. Thunder was still rumbling in the west and the sky was heavily overcast, but the rain held off.

"May work to our advantage, if it comes down hard," he thought.

When he reached town he immediately repaired to the sheriff's office. He found one of the deputies there.

"Where's Walsh?" he asked.

"Over to the Ace-Full with Kells, eatin'," said the deputy.

"Go get him and Kells and bring them here," Hatfield ordered preemptorily. The deputy immediately hurried out to perform the chore. Hatfield rolled a cigarette, sat down at the sheriff's desk and waited.

The deputy was back in short order. With him were Hugh Kells and Sheriff Walsh, the latter wiping his mustache.

"What's the big notion?" he demanded in injured tones. "Hustlin' a man away from his dinner half et? I left a full bowl of stew on the table."

"Got a chore for you," Hatfield replied. He was fumbling with a cunningly concealed secret pocket in his broad leather belt as he spoke. He laid something on the table before them.

"G-good gosh!" stuttered the deputy.

"Well, I'll be damned," said Kells.

"I might have knowed it," rumbled the sheriff.

The object on the table was a gleaming silver star set on a silver circle, the honored, feared and respected badge of the Texas Rangers.

"I might have knowed it," the sheriff repeated. "You do things like a Ranger."

Abruptly his eyes widened. "By gosh, I got yuh placed!" he burst forth. "Been wonderin' who it was I'd heard about you reminded me of. You're the Lone Wolf!"

"Been called that," Hatfield admitted.

The others stared at the almost legendary figure whose exploits were already famous from the Rio Grande to the Red River and beyond.

"The Lone Wolf," repeated the sheriff. "Bill McDowell's Lieutenant! So Captain Bill sent yuh over here, eh?"

"That's right," Hatfield replied, "in answer to a letter written by Walt Cowdry. Now, Walsh, I'm playing another hunch."

"Play it, and I'll foller it," declared the sheriff. "What yuh want me to do?"

"Get your other deputy," Hatfield directed. "We're riding. I figure the five of us will be enough and we may not have any time to waste, although I don't think anything will bust loose before daylight, especially if the rain comes on as it looks like it will."

171

As they rode out of town, Hatfield told his followers as much as he deemed necessary.

"I've a prime notion that snooper who saw me stow the image in the safe also saw me put the map back inside it," he concluded. "If he did, I figure they'll make a quick try for the gold they'll think is hid in the cave. I feel they're getting pretty jittery and will want to make a good haul and pull out of the section. Things haven't been going well for them of late. They put one over on me this time, all right. I didn't keep as close a watch on the mine workers as I should have. They evidently had one more jigger planted there and he was keeping close tabs on me all the time. But it may work out for the best after all."

They paused at the Tumbling K ranchhouse and found the watchman okay. He reported that nothing had happened during Hatfield's absence.

"That helps," the Lone Wolf said. "The chances are they won't get there ahead of us as they would have if they were forced to enter the canyon by the mouth. I felt pretty sure when I was up at the head of the gorge that there were ways into the valley by way of the northern slopes. They're all split up by side canyons and gulches. Doubtless

172

there's a trail from the east through one or another of them. So I'm hoping they will hold off so they'll hit the canyon after daylight. I'd say they have done considerable snooping around the upper end of the valley, but with that tangle of draws and brakes up there their search was practically hopeless till they got hold of the map. That would tell them just about where to look, but they couldn't hope to spot the place in the dark on a rainy night."

"Sounds reasonable," admitted the sheriff. "Hope you're right."

"I'd better be," Hatfield predicted grimly. "If they are already there, holed up and waiting for daylight, we may get a reception we won't like. We'll have to take it careful and easy after we get well up the valley. Can't afford the chance of running into a drygulching."

The sky was gray with approaching dawn when they reached the box end of the canyon after a cautious advance for the last few miles. All was silent and apparently deserted. The rain had begun to fall and clouds of mist swirled and eddied in the narrow gorge.

Drenched by the rain and chilled by the wind that soughed down the gorge, they concealed their horses nearby and took up uncomfortable positions of concealment in the growth close to the cliff face.

Slowly the light grew stronger, but the rain and the mist made everything appear grotesque and unreal. The roar of the fall sounded hollowly, a deep undertone to the swish of the rain and the thin wailing of the wind.

An hour passed with the wind steadily rising and the rain coming down harder. The mist clouds filled the canyon to the brim. The chimney rocks and clumps of growth became weird forms that seemed to writhe with tortured life. The scene was unreal, a formless inferno where time stood still and merged with the endless void of eternity.

"Get set!" Hatfield suddenly whispered. "They're coming!"

Shadowy shapes appeared from down canyon. They resolved into five horsemen riding slowly toward the pluming fall with peering eyes. They pulled up not ten yards distant.

Jim Hatfield stepped into view. On his broad breast gleamed the star of the Rangers. His face was set in bleak lines, his eyes were coldly gray as the misted granite of the canyon walls. He had a quick glimpse of the giant, red-haired Purdy, of Shelton, the former mill foreman, of a lean little rat of a man he instantly recognized as one of the mine laborers, and of Bern Cowdry's devilishly handsome, rage-distorted face. His voice rolled in thunder above the roar of the falls and the hiss of the wind-driven rain —

"In the name of the State of Texas! I arrest Bern Cowdry and others for robbery and murder. Anything you say —"

His voice was drowned by a bellow of gunfire as owlhoots and possemen went into action. Shooting with both hands, he saw Purdy reel and fall. He saw the treacherous mine worker go down. Two more men had their hands in the air and were howling for mercy.

Bern Cowdry, shooting and cursing, whirled his tall black horse and went charging down the canyon, lead hissing all around him. A split second and the swirling mist had swallowed him up.

Hatfield bounded to where Goldy stood. He flung himself into the saddle and sent the great sorrel racing in pursuit.

Over the stones they flew, branches raking them, the rain lashing them like liquid whips. Ahead was only the writhing mist wreaths, the grotesque chimney rocks and the bristle of thickets.

But Hatfield knew the fugitive would have

to stick to the creek bank. Elsewhere the growth was too thick, the ground too littered with huge boulders. He bent low in the saddle, stuffing fresh cartridges into the cylinders of his guns and peering ahead.

They covered a mile, with death or broken bones promised with every straining leap of the great golden horse. The better part of another mile and Hatfield began to wonder if Cowdry had turned off by way of some secret track he knew.

And then through the mist and rain showed a vague shape speeding south. It was the black horse and its rider.

Hatfield's voice rang out, urgent, compelling —

"Trail, Goldy, trail!"

The sorrel responded with a gallant burst of speed. His irons clanged on the stones, showering sparks, his powerful legs shot backward like pistons as he fairly poured his long body over the ground. Slowly but surely he closed the distance.

A bullet whined past Hatfield's face. The report, dull and hollow, was swept away on the wind. Another slug, closer this time. But the Ranger grimly held his fire. He had a glimpse of the white blur that was Bern Cowdry's distorted face.

The great black horse was giving its best,

but it was not enough. Slowly, the racing sorrel closed in. Hatfield reached for his guns.

Abruptly Bern Cowdry gave up the race. He jerked his mount to a slithering, stumbling halt, whirled him "on a dime" and faced his pursuer, guns roaring.

Hatfield also pulled up. Shot for shot he answered the owlhoot's fire. The horses plunged and snorted as the guns roared. Their riders were flickering, swaying shadows blasting death at one another through the veil of the mist and the rain.

Hatfield felt the burn of a bullet along his cheek. Another nicked his shoulder. A third ripped the sleeve of his shirt. He steadied Goldy with a word and pressed both triggers, his guns clamped rock-steady against his hips.

Bern Cowdry screamed, a scream of rage and pain and terror that ended in a bubbling shriek. He strove to raise his guns for a last shot, but they dropped from his nerveless hands. He lurched sideways, plunged to the ground, writhed an instant and was still.

Hatfield got stiffly from the saddle. With slow steps he walked to the side of the fallen outlaw, gun ready for instant action. Then he holstered it and stood staring down at the quiet form. Bern Cowdry was dead.

A moment later, Sheriff Walsh and Hugh Kells dashed up. The other had been left to guard the two prisoners.

"Bern Cowdry," said the sheriff, shaking his head over the quiet form. "I'd never have believed it. He seemed a real sort of feller. Gambled a good deal and drank some. But those are the things yuh expect a young feller to do. Well, blood will tell. His dad took the wrong trail when he was young. Pore Walt never could do anything with Chet. Walt was steady-goin', Chet was just the opposite. Well, it happens everywhere, but it's a pity."

They rode back up the canyon. While the sheriff looked over the dead men, Hatfield questioned the two prisoners. With visions of dancing on nothing at the end of a rope, the owlhoots talked freely and told him all they knew.

"I got the whole thing pretty well pieced together," Hatfield told Walsh and Kells. "Old Miguel was one of a bunch Bern Cowdry worked with over in Arizona before things got too hot to hold them there, although, like Cowdry he originally came from this section. He had that golden image. Reckon it came down through his family. The legend of Moon Valley came along with it. Miguel knew the map was inside the image and knew something was hidden in the valley, he didn't know just what. He figured it must be a store of gold buried by the old Aztec priests.

"But Miguel was superstitious. He was nearly all Indian, of the old Aztec blood, and he feared the concentrated curse of the evil Aztec gods the priests promised for anyone revealing the secret to someone of alien blood, meaning chiefly, of course, the Teules, as the Aztecs named the Spanish invaders. So Miguel never dared make a try for the treasure he thought was here."

"Then how did Cowdry catch onto it?" Kells asked as Hatfield paused to roll a cigarette.

Hatfield gestured to one of the prisoners. "That little one there with Shelton is also half Indian," he explained. "Miguel told him something about it — not all. He merely told him there was much gold hidden in Moon Valley. That feller wasn't scared of the old gods like Miguel was. He told Bern Cowdry what Miguel said. Cowdry believed him and immediately set out to get hold of Moon Valley. He figured that what Miguel was talking about was a rich gold ledge. Kells making his strike in the mouth of the valley tended to corroborate the notion. But meanwhile Cowdry set the other half-Indian to watch Miguel and try and learn more."

"And he found out Miguel had the image?"

Hatfield pinched out his cigarette butt and cast it aside.

"That's right," he replied. "He didn't learn the secret of the image, but he was smart enough to figure it contained the secret in one way or other. So they decided to kill Miguel and get it.

"But Miguel caught on and hightailed. They lit out after him and trailed him into the desert. Were closing in on him, but that darn rattlesnake beat them to it, and then I came along. Miguel was grateful to me for what I did for him, and I reckon, too, he figured it was a chance to doublecross the bunch that doublecrossed him. So he gave me the image. He tried hard to tell me about it, but died before he could get the words out."

Hatfield rolled another cigarette, his eyes thoughtful.

"A good example of crooked owlhoot thinking," he concluded. "The sort of thing that, sooner or later, always causes them to make the slips that are their undoing. They were doing pretty well by themselves in this section, but they couldn't be satisfied. Had to be reaching out for more. Bern Cowdry was always in debt, of course, through his gambling. He had a first-rate chance of sharing in his uncle's holdings if he'd gone straight after he came back here, but he had to go after what he considered was easy money."

"Easy money is usually mighty hard money before yuh finish with it," the sheriff observed sententiously. "I reckon Bern did for Walt Cowdry, too, eh?"

"So Shelton told me," Hatfield replied. "Shelton said Bern and his uncle had a final grand row over Bern's gambling and that his uncle ordered him off the place. So he killed Walt Cowdry in a way that would throw suspicion on Kells. He knew, of course, that if he was forced to sever connections with the Cross C, he couldn't carry on in the section any longer. The Cross C was his cover-up and a plumb perfect one."

"Suppose Purdy and Shelton and that other one were part of his Arizona bunch?" remarked Kells.

"That's so," Hatfield said. "By the way, did Bern Cowdry recommend one of those jiggers to you?"

"By gosh, he did," Kells replied. "He recommended Purdy as a first-rate hard rock man when I was lookin' for somebody to take the place of my first drill foreman who didn't show up one day. It had plumb slipped my mind till right now."

"Chances are they did for your former foreman to make way for Purdy," Hatfield conjectured. "We'll ask about that later. Well, reckon we might as well be headed for town with that pair. I'll be riding on this evening. Looks like the rain is letting up. Captain Bill will have another little chore lined up for me by the time I get back to the Post. I'll try that short-cut across the desert again. Should be cooler at night after the rain. Sorry I can't stay for the wedding, Kells. Tell Mary hello for me, and the best of luck to you both."

They watched him ride away some hours later, the red rays of the setting sun etching his sternly handsome profile in flame, a look of quiet content and pleased anticipation in his strangely colored eyes.

"And there," Kells remarked to Sheriff Walsh, "goes a man!"

"Uh-huh," the sheriff agreed soberly, "one of the reasons the Rangers are the *Rangers!* Let's go eat."

ABOUT THE AUTHOR

Leslie Scott was born in Lewisburg, West Virginia. During the Great War, he joined the French Foreign Legion and spent four years in the trenches. In the 1920s he worked as a mining engineer and bridge builder in the western American states and in China before settling in New York. A barroom discussion in 1934 with Leo Margulies, who was managing editor for Standard Magazines, prompted Scott to try writing fiction. He went on to create two of the most notable series characters in Western pulp magazines. In 1936, Standard Magazines launched, and in *Texas Rangers,* Scott under the house name of **Jackson Cole** created Jim Hatfield, Texas Ranger, a character whose popularity was so great with readers that this magazine featuring his adventures lasted until 1958. When others eventually began contributing Jim Hatfield stories, Scott created another Texas Ranger hero,

Walt Slade, better known as *El Halcon,* the Hawk, whose exploits were regularly featured in *Thrilling Western.* In the 1950s Scott moved quickly into writing book-length adventures about both Jim Hatfield and Walt Slade in long series of original paperback Westerns. At the same time, however, Scott was also doing some of his best work in hardcover Westerns published by Arcadia House; thoughtful, well-constructed stories, with engaging characters and authentic settings and situations. Among the best of these, surely, are *Silver City* (1953), *Longhorn Empire* (1954), *The Trail Builders* (1956), and *Blood on the Rio Grande* (1959). In these hardcover Westerns, many of which have never been reprinted, Scott proved himself highly capable of writing traditional Western stories with characters who have sufficient depth to change in the course of the narrative and with a degree of authenticity and historical accuracy absent from many of his series stories.

We hope you have enjoyed this Large Print book. Other Thorndike, Wheeler, and Chivers Press Large Print books are available at your library or directly from the publishers.

For information about current and upcoming titles, please call or write, without obligation, to:

Publisher
Thorndike Press
295 Kennedy Memorial Drive
Waterville, ME 04901
Tel. (800) 223-1244

or visit our Web site at:

http://gale.cengage.com/thorndike

OR

Chivers Large Print
published by BBC Audiobooks Ltd
St James House, The Square
Lower Bristol Road
Bath BA2 3SB
England
Tel. +44(0) 800 136919
email: bbcaudiobooks@bbc.co.uk
www.bbcaudiobooks.co.uk

All our Large Print titles are designed for easy reading, and all our books are made to last.